About the Author

Max V. Carp calls Los Angeles his home. His award-winning short fiction has appeared in *Inscape*, *SLAB Literary Magazine*, *The Sunspot Literary Journal*, *Narrative*, and elsewhere. A section of this novel has appeared in a different form in *SLAB*.

The Cali Book of the Dead

Max V. Carp

The Cali Book of the Dead

Vanguard Press

VANGUARD PAPERBACK

© Copyright 2024
Max V. Carp

The right of Max V. Carp to be identified as author of
this work has been asserted by him in accordance with the
Copyright, Designs and Patents Act 1988.

All Rights Reserved

No reproduction, copy or transmission of this publication
may be made without written permission.
No paragraph of this publication may be reproduced,
copied or transmitted save with the written permission of the
publisher, or in accordance with the provisions
of the Copyright Act 1956 (as amended).

Any person who commits any unauthorised act in relation to
this publication may be liable to criminal
prosecution and civil claims for damages.

A CIP catalogue record for this title is
available from the British Library.

ISBN 978 1 80016 655 4

This is a work of fiction. Names, characters, businesses, places, events and
incidents are either the product of the author's imagination or used in a
fictitious manner. Any resemblance to actual persons, living or dead, or
actual events is purely coincidental.

Vanguard Press is an imprint of
Pegasus Elliot Mackenzie Publishers Ltd.
www.pegasuspublishers.com

First Published in 2024

Vanguard Press
Sheraton House Castle Park
Cambridge England

Printed & Bound in Great Britain

For Colin and Denis

*"Now the time has come
 for you
  to seek a path."*

The Tibetan Book of the Dead, Day One

In the pitch-dark room, there are signs of life. A deep sigh flushes out like the last words of a mute. The mattress squeaks, followed shortly by light footsteps and then complete silence, that grim augury before a major earthquake, which is what that moment feels like to him, a lifelong Los Angeleno.

He parts the drapes, and a flood of California sunlight nearly blinds him where he stands. He shields his eyes in defense, annoyed by the intrusion in what would otherwise have been a rather complacent state of mind. He can read the signs when he's dialed in, as he is now, and he's quickly overcome by the portents of a nefarious presence floating in the air around him, an Asura monster poking at the outer edge of the visible world.

Perhaps another fateful day for Landon Briggs, in other words.

Well into his forties, Landon fancies himself a man of the world. There's an "Om" tattoo on his neck, forming the centerpiece in a flower-of-life type of symbol. He got the seed of that tattoo not long before he left the roost and went to conquer the world. He was about sixteen at the time, give or take, lived for rock 'n' roll, and thought, with the innocence of youth, that a sound-of-the-universe symbol on his neck would curry favor with the music gods. That wasn't the craziest thought to ever cross his mind.

He's constantly worked at embellishing the tattoo and, if not for time, it'd probably end up covering his entire body like some kind of Buddhist version of the Illustrated Man.

"What'd you tell him?" Landon asks the naked woman lying in bed.

He turns to study her as she picks her clothes up off the floor, the light making her look like a Greek goddess in some bucolic Arcadian landscape. Melanie looks even better now, he reckons, than when they first met eighteen years ago. Man, how time flies. The blink of an eye in the grand scheme of things, yet a span of time containing most of his adult life. Major events nestled in like rosary beads: one for their brief courtship; one for the birth of their first son, Jason; one for the wedding; one for the birth of their second son, Tyler; one for Jason's death; one for the divorce, and now yet another bead for Mel's engagement to a man he loathed.

"The truth," Melanie says. "Had to go to a funeral."

"I'm sure my old man appreciates that, wherever he is," Landon says. "Thanks for coming."

"Someone had to," she says.

Funerals always fill Landon with a sense of embarrassment he can't quite place, and his father's funeral was no different. It's almost as if Landon feels shame for the deceased, like they've suddenly lost their jobs and are soon found roaming down Skid Row at night, glugging a slug of Skol out of a brown bag. A change of status that Landon doesn't want to be associated with, as he's always learned to keep it *positive*, if only to alleviate the feeling of being constantly cursed. But it's not that, of course. It's just fear. Overwhelming fear.

"Y'know, I been thinking," Landon says, and watches Melanie recoil, immediately assuming an en garde stance with that last word of his, *thinking*. "Don't marry that guy. I wanna come back home. A boy should grow up with his dad, don't you think?"

"Never mind Tyler, don't bring him into this," Melanie says.

"His birthday's coming up, when, Tuesday?"

"Wednesday."

"Yeah, Wednesday," Landon says. "Let's spend it together, way we used to."

"Did you get him something?"

"Course," Landon lies. "It's a surprise."

Melanie rolls her eyes, accustomed as she is to his equivocating ways. She moves her hair out of the way as she fastens her bra.

"Okay, never mind Tyler," he continues. "This guy you're gonna marry, you ever have any doubts about him?"

She points to the bed like a police detective would the scene of the crime. "What do you think *this* was all about?" She comes up behind him real close, not hugging or anything, just stands there and Landon again feels that warmth between them, like a tangible physical presence with a consciousness of its own, although he couldn't tell if it was birthing itself on the spot or if it was something recalled from happier times or going back even further to a prophetic dream he once had, not that it made any difference to him.

"Do me a favor, don't tell Tyler about my ol' man," Landon says. "He never even met him, y'know. Don't feel like answering a thousand questions about the afterlife."

As they shuffle into the sparsely furnished living room of this two-bedroom apartment in Sherman Oaks, Melanie reaches for an envelope resting on the IKEA coffee table and hands it to Landon. He still receives the occasional mail at this, his old address, and he duly picks it up on his weekly visits to his son. Landon takes a quick glance at the envelope. Probably some junk mail from the Army, he guesses, seeing as he forgot to tell 'em he got kicked out of his own house. He rips the envelope open only to quickly realize that the letter is anything but junk. It has the official 'Department of the Army, Headquarters California Army National Guard' header, addressed Memorandum to Landon Kennen Briggs, so there's no mistake about it. Landon's eyes quickly slip down the page as his worst nightmare is confirmed. He's heard rumors of ex-soldiers having been asked by the Army to pay back their reenlistment bonus, but thought it was some kind of mistake, that something like that could never happen in this day and age. And yet there it is, a letter to the effect that he has to pay back his $21,000 bonus, the very reason he went back to that Middle Eastern hellhole in the first place. The letter states that the payment was made in violation of DoD guidance, and in violation of federal law, as if it was Landon's fault that he was offered the money. The sheer injustice of the bait-and-switch ruse leaves Landon frozen. His mind is racing to images of carnage and mayhem, all within state limits.

* * *

Tyler's room is a shrine to horses. Pictures, Pony Express posters, netsuke, even a used old saddle, a movie prop Landon found at the flea market on Fairfax and Melrose. He asked the seller for a certificate of authenticity, but none was forthcoming, and with his son crying his heart out for everyone to see what a neglected little squirt he was, Landon reluctantly shelled out the money. A few days later, he caught that Western on late-night cable and suffered through two hours of gay cowpokes spewing stilted lines but, to him, spotting his saddle was like looking for a stolen bike in Tiananmen Square.

Tyler has his earbuds on, a Greek mythology book on his lap, his mind completely immersed. He looks preppy, with his reading glasses, a button-down shirt, khakis, and a V-neck vest, a look Landon doesn't approve of but has to concede matches Tyler's temperament and general disposition. Kind of kid would get the crap beaten outta him on a daily basis back when Landon was in school. Nothing about Tyler resembled the ease and insouciant spirit of his late brother, Jason, who despite the cloud of uncertainty hovering over his later years decided to make his days count, an attitude which Jason followed almost all the way up to the day he died. Landon committed that tragic day to memory in its utmost detail, something to be regorged from time to time and lived over again, as if to unravel its meaning, a perennial mystery never to be mentioned to another living soul. He will take that secret to the grave, but Tyler, the direct beneficiary of that particular guilt trip, was consequently bestowed with a fatherly love bordering on obsession. Though, clearly, no obsession to detail, as Landon sees himself as more of a "big picture" kinda guy.

Landon removes Tyler's earbuds, startling him out of his reverie. "C'mon, bud, they're about to open the gates," he says. He shuffles Tyler out the door, lagging behind just enough for an aside with Melanie. "Hey, Mel, can you do me a favor? I didn't get a chance to swing by the bank this morning."

"Sixty okay?" she asks, springing for her wallet.

"You mind?" Landon says, grabbing the cash like yet another lifeline, already thinking of getting himself in a more favorable position vis a vis that new debt.

* * *

The Santa Anita horse racetrack has always held a special place in Landon's heart. It's been the scene of some of his most glorious moments, stories he's kept repeating ad nauseam, constantly embellishing them until even *he* started questioning their veracity. Alas, it's also the place that has seen the worst of Landon, days he'd rather forget. The days he lost money, and there were plenty of those, didn't bother Landon in the least, as he has no attachment to accumulating wealth, or even something much simpler, like a nest egg. No, what really messes with his head is that empty feeling the morning after a big win, the moment he realizes that, if he set his mind to it, he could have every little thing in the world and yet could never have it *all*. He sees himself as a mythical lion taking a bite out of Earth, wanting to relish every flavor, every feeling, every thought, all there is to know in this realm of experience.

He wants to swallow the Moon and spit out the Sun.

Landon shows Tyler how to fill out a racing form, but the kid finds it hard going, like he's running on diesel fuel or something. The child nods like a good soldier, and Landon slams sixty bucks on the counter to announce his presence in the great hall. Soon as he gets his tickets, he has Tyler kiss them for good luck, and that finally gets the boy going.

Landon loves his son to death, and he lives for moments like this, which he archives away like a diligent librarian. While not overly attentive to the particulars—he once got Tyler the wrong and, dammit, non-refundable prescription glasses—he does remember each and every experience they shared. Landon likes to recall a story he once heard from an itinerant Buddhist monk, or whatever his correct nomenclature was, down at the Venice Beach Boardwalk. The monk showed him a crystal-like bead that he carried in a small velvety pouch and said, with an authority beyond Landon's ability to fully comprehend, that it was one of the most prized relics to be found on earth. "It is called a *śarīra*," the monk said. "The *śarīras* are to be found in the cremated remains of the great Buddhist masters," he said, as if reciting from some holy book, and then held the sacred object in the sunlight for emphasis. "They cannot be found in the ashes of ordinary folks like you because, you see, the *śarīras* are made up of elements *not* of this earth."

After much cajoling, the monk let him touch the *śarīra*, but to Landon's disappointment, it felt no different than rubbing a glass bead. Just the same, the story stayed with Landon, and he's come to think of his entire life boiling down to the times spent together with his wife and sons, his only *śarīras* able to survive the cauldron of his tumultuous existence. That's the essence of his journey through life, he figures, and as a general rule to live by, he staunchly refuses to identify with the job title on his business card or some such staples of societal status. Not that he's had either of those lately, job or business card, mere details for a man not inclined to get bogged down by technicalities, except perhaps for those of a philosophical nature.

Tyler has a mark on his forehead from pressing too hard against the rail, sticking his little arm out to touch the galloping thoroughbreds, like so many purple unicorns, as they warm up before the race. "They go by too fast, Daddy," Tyler says, nearly dropping his ice-cream cone. It takes Landon a second to realize he's talking about horses and not another *śarīra* in the making.

Landon takes Tyler on a spontaneous tour of the quarters, filling in the dead time with stories about the rules of the game, and how they name horses and how the meaning of those names oftentimes decides a horse's fate before even running a single race. *Much like with people*, he figures, but keeps that to himself. He then walks Tyler into a stable for the big reveal and watches the boy's face drop as he realizes that there was nothing impromptu about their tour. Landon introduces the boy to his old buddy, Big Ben, a jockey he's met in AA a lifetime ago, and his racehorse "The Lion's Den".

"How you feelin', Ben?" Landon asks.

"Feelin' pretty good. If I were you, I'd bet everything on this guy," Ben says.

"Not crazy about the name, 'The Lion's Den.' Like my life's in danger or something," Landon says.

"Kinda name makes you think," Big Ben says. He sizes Tyler up, the two looking like classmates height-wise, ages apart in worldliness. "This your other boy, right? About time."

"Yeah, man, he loves horses worse than Jason did," Landon says.

Big Ben runs a brush on the side of the horse. "What's your name, son?" he asks.

"Tyler," he says in a near-whisper, as he always reverts to a low voice whenever his dead brother's name is mentioned, as if afraid to wake his ghost. "Don't be shy," Big Ben says, and grabs Tyler's hand and runs it over the side of the horse and then over his wet nostrils. "He likes it when you do that," Big Ben says, "Can you feel his breath?" For Tyler it feels like a communion of sorts, completely natural yet far removed from his daily experience. "And if you ever dreamed of—" Big Ben is about to ask, when Tyler curtly cuts him off.

"I don't dream."

Big Ben looks at Landon for an explanation, but he just shrugs it off. "I haven't dreamed in two years, eleven months, and twenty-six days," Tyler says matter-of-factly.

Big Ben (not so) quickly does the math in his head, and Landon nods at him to confirm his unspoken conclusion. It has indeed been that long since Jason passed away. Landon gets a jump on the situation, wanting to keep the spirit of the moment light and fun. "You wanna get up on him, Tyler?" The boy is game and Big Ben gets one of Tyler's feet up on the stirrup, is about to lift him up on the saddle, when he hears a familiar voice booming over his right shoulder.

"My horse just got over a case of the colic, now you've turned him into the main attraction at a petting zoo?" the intruder bellows.

Big Ben brings Tyler back down to earth, literally, and turns his full attention to his employer, Mr. Rocanna.

"Mr. Rocanna... Sorry, sir, I just—"

"Outta the way," Mr. Rocanna says. A middle-aged man dressed in a crisp white suit, knee-high leather boots, straw Panama hat, he hops on the horse like he owns it, which he does. The wall behind is painted pale blue, and the man appears like a war hero from a middle-aged painting, rallying his troops against the backdrop of an innocent azure sky.

Landon is suddenly overwhelmed by a feeling of déjà vu at the sight of Mr. Rocanna. He's seen him around the course and up in the club, has spoken to him on several occasions, the conversations always taking strange turns into the abstract, but doesn't recall ever seeing him in the barn. And yet, the feeling is unmistakable, and Landon feels a rush of nausea take over him.

Mr. Rocanna leans forward, as if to listen to the horse. While deep in the metaphysical quicksand, Landon hears Mr. Rocanna's words before they are even uttered. The sounds come at him from all sides, front, back, above, and below, all at the same time, disorienting Landon into paralysis. "You people got him spooked," he says, before singling Big Ben out. "Make sure you loosen him up before the race."

"Yes sir," Big Ben says, all business now.

Landon looks away from the blue aura enveloping Mr. Rocanna and glances in the direction of the white light coming in through the barn and leading up to the track. He quickly regains his balance, just in time to notice the confusion on Tyler's face, a sense of disappointment difficult to hide. "The gentleman owns this beautiful horse," he says to his son, in the way of explaining the balance of power. "I got your horse singled, Mr. Rocanna. Put all our money on it—" Landon says, like it was some kind of accomplishment. "Didn't we, Tyler?"

Mr. Rocanna whispers something in the horse's ear and the horse turns its head, one big eye fixed on Landon. Mr. Rocanna sits back up straight on the saddle, his eyes glowering down on Landon, who must feel like he is looking up at the marble statue of a vengeful god, or an avatar to say the least. That spooks Landon and Tyler both.

"Oh, they're still here?" Mr. Rocanna says to Big Ben, meaning Landon and Tyler. The child looks down, embarrassed. He tries to gently nudge his dad out of an increasingly uncomfortable situation.

"Wait now, sir, we didn't come here to—" Landon says, just as a bell sounds in the distance.

"Did you hear that bell? Means it's time for you to go gamble away your rent money," Mr. Rocanna says.

"Okay, I see what you're doing," Landon says, spotting another ruined moment in the rearview mirror. Big Ben grimaces at him, in the way of an apology.

"A nice lesson to teach your child. I see the likes of you here all the time, and I know all about you in particular," Mr. Rocanna continues. "Don't act so surprised."

"We have to leave now, Tyler," Landon says, but his body doesn't follow his mind's command.

"What is your name, young boy?"

"Tyler Gordon Briggs."

"Well, Tyler Gordon Briggs, the reason I'm sitting up here is because I have a nose for winners, a flair that extends, many would agree, to people. And in your father I've seen, in our past conversations, albeit few and far between, that rare sparkle in the eyes. You know the kind I'm talking about? The spirit struggling in human form. The spark of life, the pneuma of *Deus absconditus* for us grown-ups. Look at this horse here, a beautiful animal, but study its face closer and what do you see?" Mr. Rocanna asks. Tyler follows his instructions and studies the horse's face, momentarily getting lost in the dark of its eyes. "*Dead eyes!*" Mr. Rocanna exclaims. "Look at Big Ben now, a winning jockey and honorable drunk, but take a closer look. *Dead eyes*." Big Ben nods in agreement, resigned to his fate, as Mr. Rocanna carries on. "But your father, Tyler, is a different breed. He's at heart a street philosopher, the best kind of philosopher, and yet he's wasting his life away at the tracks. I think he ought to know better, lest you, young stud, wish to continue his legacy. Like father, like son. And is there any reason in the world why you might want for that, my dear Tyler Gordon Briggs?" Mr. Rocanna says.

The child shakes his head, near to tears, and looks down. "I wanna go home now, Dad," he says, gently tugging at his sleeve. Landon kisses his son the way he's done so often in the past when Tyler would hurt himself during a game of catch, or fall off his bike and get a bruise, but this time it feels different. Landon looks at his boy and realizes that the walls surrounding his innocence have just caved in, that the child standing in front of him is not the child he'd brought to the track that morning. That child has died to childhood.

At the same time, Landon can't help but notice that something inside *himself* turned too. He's heard the type of cautionary words spewed from the mouth of Mr. Rocanna before, as he's been the subject of many such well-meaning yet ineffective interventions. The weight of Mr. Rocanna's words, mere platitudes in another context, register not in the words themselves but in the whole experience, which Landon suffers through to the innermost particle of his being. It's that rare time where the lines between the physical, the moral, and the spiritual are completely blurred. Matter of fact, Landon has to think back to reassure himself that the whole thing wasn't just the effect of some late-kicking pill someone might have popped into his mouth the night before, which incidentally is also a blur.

* * *

Landon and Tyler walk hand in hand toward the exit gates, looking for all the world like the child is dragging his own dad out of the principal's office.

Nick, a scraggly old man, looking like he's just crawled out of a sewer, bursts through the turnstiles like *he* is a racehorse. "Damn, Landon, how'd you go broke before the first race? Must be some kind of record, even for you," he says at the sight of Landon leaving prematurely.

Landon pulls his betting slips out and shoves them into Nick's hand, more like dropping them there from a safe distance. "Good luck, Nick!"

"What I owe you, Landon?"

"Nothing. Nada. Free as in beer."

"Free! Shit, man, that's like my *second* favorite word in the English language," Nick says, looking every bit like he could use a freebie.

* * *

"Had fun at the park, Tyler?" Melanie asks, but all she hears is the sound of the bedroom door closing behind the boy.

"I think he's coming down with a cold or something. Been cranky all day," Landon says. "I don't know what's gotten into him."

"Can you watch him the rest of the evening?" Melanie asks.

"Naw, I gotta go see Frankie about something," Landon says. "Why?"

"I got a shipment of cigarettes coming in," Melanie says.

"When?"

"Four o'clock."

"See what I mean, this Ray guy's a fuckin' prick. Makes you work on a holiday week—," Landon says, censoring himself at the last moment.

"It's not a real holiday, Halloween," Melanie says, "And it shouldn't last a whole week." She stammers, like she can't let go of this thought. "I-I-I wish this whole Halloween went to fucking hell!"

"Forget it," Landon jumps in, like tip toeing around a tender subject. "I just meant, don't know what you're doing with him. Honest."

Melanie lets her thoughts run for some time, her face twitching in strange ways. At last, she says, "He promised me health insurance."

Landon rolls his head back in a dramatic gesture, like someone just laid a trump card on the table, leaving him to count his losses. "Well, can't beat that." Looks like she's heard enough already, and she opens the front door for Landon to take a hint.

"You see the price of cigarettes lately?" Landon thinks out loud. "That load must be worth a million bucks, huh?"

"That's why I have to be there myself, make sure it doesn't end up in the wrong hands," she says.

"That liquor truck got boosted last year, word on the street is Ray did it himself. With the help of the Diadora brothers, of course, 'cause he's too big of a pussy. Oh, yeah. Sold the goods to a Chinese fence and later collected on the insurance, doubled up on it. Way to pay for a fancy wedding." Landon takes a step back as if to avoid the shrapnel.

"Forgive me if I don't believe the *word on the street*."

"He's just another crook, Mel. No better'n me. You best believe it."

"Prove it," she says, as she cants her head slightly.

"Oh, you mean if I were to show up here tomorrow with a million bucks, you'd send Ray packing and give me a second chance?" Landon asks.

"I'm open to miracles. It's always been my policy," she says, to effectively close the conversation. "Go, now. Your friends must think you're dead."

* * *

It's a long drive downtown, hitting the I-5 southbound at peak hour, which only makes Mr. Rocanna's putdown earlier in the day come back into Landon's head like a killing fields buzzard. It really stuck in Landon's crop, and it bothers him that Tyler's gonna remember this incident for the rest of his life, being old enough to retain these kinds of memories. Matter of fact, to this day Landon still holds a vivid recollection of a particularly savage beating he once received, courtesy of his own dad, when he was about Tyler's age. He'd asked his old man to let him move in with his mom, and Mr. Briggs's resentment toward his ex-wife came to a boiling point. The belt was Mr Briggs's (he demanded that his son call him "Mr. Briggs") weapon of choice, and the metal buckle left two thick scars, like an *X*, on Landon's back. "*X* marks the spot," his old man used to joke afterwards whenever Landon inquired about his mother's whereabouts. "She doesn't want you, she doesn't want *us*. Get used to it," he'd say. A couple years later, he overheard Mr. Briggs talk about her in hushed tones with some of his friends during a Fourth of July barbecue at the house. It turned out she'd died of some disease or other; Landon never asked, disappointed as he was with her for abandoning him at the crossroads. In the intervening years, her image slowly faded in Landon's mind, and with nary a photograph to jog his memory, she became as immaterial as a notion, an idea of something that consumed him for not understanding it, yet another hungry ghost in his life.

* * *

A few months prior to Mr. Briggs' passing, Landon got a call from Cedars Sinai to come pick up his father, as he was unfit to drive himself home after a round of radiation therapy. It took Landon a few moments to string up the chain of events that led up to that call. He hadn't seen or spoken to his dad in years and was actually surprised to hear that he was still alive. Mr. Briggs *was* dying, it turned out, of lung cancer by way of a two-pack a day smoking habit that he'd maintained religiously throughout his adult life (which by his own account started at fourteen, as was the norm in the olden days in Bunz Town, Nebraska). The old man put Landon's name and phone number down as the emergency contact on the hospital form knowing full well that Landon would take pity on him in the hope of settling some old scores.

Landon recognized his dad's old red plaid shirt first before acknowledging the wraith inhabiting the space within. They didn't speak while Landon loaded him up like a piece of fragile luggage into his car and quickly got onto Beverly heading East toward the 101 Freeway. The quiet unsettled Landon and he kept bobbing his head up and down to a silent tune in his head. It was a nervous tic left over from the days he'd go around wearing massive headphones at all times, blasting heavy metal straight into his astral body.

Mr. Briggs pulled out a cigarette and lit up with trembling hands. "Hope you don't mind," he said, breaking the silence.

Landon kept shaking his head as the old man took a deep puff. Landon snatched the pack of cigarettes out of his dad's hand and tossed it in the back seat.

"Won't make no goddamn difference anyhow—," Mr. Briggs grunted, before bursting into a coughing fit. When he settled down a bit he reached into his pocket and took out a couple of small trinkets.

"Went back to Vietnam last year," he said. "Got this thing here for your son, he's how old now, seven or eight? Boy loves his horses, don't he... Saw that on the social media and whatnot."

Landon held the trinket, turned it over, like something was missing from the picture. "What's this?"

"It's some kinda Tibetan spirit horse, or something," Mr. Briggs said.

"What do you mean?"

"I don't know, I'm just telling you what I was told. Maybe it was all bullshit, ha-ha, joke's on me."

"What do they call it?"

"It's a Tibetan horse, son, that's all I know. You asking me what his name is in... *American*? I don't know, call him what you want. Can't you just accept a present without asking me a million questions? Tell your son it's from his granddad, who got it from a Tibetan monk in Vietnam. That's the story. Tell him that."

Mr. Briggs then took the second trinket, a bobblehead Buddha, and placed it on Landon's dashboard, a wicked glint in his eyes. "Ain't that the damndest thing, huh? *Same* monk sold it to me, for a pack of Marlboros," Mr. Briggs said, and started laughing, then coughing, then laughing again. "No reason to hate that place… Vietnam… no reason at all." Landon's head bobbed up and down in sync with the bobblehead for a moment before checking himself, feeling stupid all of a sudden for being cut down to the size of a toy.

Landon dropped his dad off at his rent control apartment on Alameda, close to Chinatown, about where East meets West within the city walls.

"I didn't know any better I'd tell you to stay outta trouble," Mr. Briggs said. He thanked him for the ride and told him he'd call if he needed him, but never did, and with that Landon was summarily dismissed.

Next time Landon saw his dad was at the funeral, where he couldn't help feeling regret over tossing the horse trinket in the nearest garbage can along with the dashboard bobblehead Buddha and Mr. Briggs' unused pack of cigarettes. Thing is, he wanted no link to the long line of cursed and short-lived Briggs males but that act of defiance now registered as sacrilegious, save for the pack of cigarettes, which ended up pretty much where they belonged. Landon kicked himself for acting on impulse, as he would've liked Tyler to have something to remember his grandpa by. If nothing else, a worthless toy and a cool little story to go with it can go a long way towards explaining a man to a child. The boy's imagination, Landon thought, would take over and save him the trouble of answering a bunch of stupid questions. Aside from that, Landon could've really used a dashboard Buddha. He envied the genius that invented that trinket.

* * *

Landon decides to stop worrying about all that crap and start daydreaming, a favorite pastime of his when under duress. He knows from experience that if he keeps his main consciousness occupied long enough it loses its vigilance as the mind's gatekeeper and allows other thoughts, the kind unreachable via mere reason, to manifest. And so he starts spinning a stream of consciousness out of whatever's available, contemplating the otherworldly quality of light dispersing behind the palm trees on the side of the road, say, before allowing himself to wonder about the state of the earth beneath him, its history and its memory of ancient times, of the people who wandered these lands before him, of their fates and their imprint upon this earth, of the blood they spilled and the nature of that blood, a kind of condensation of the light of the sun, he figures, though not our familiar galactic sun but a hidden black sun, calling out to him from beyond, and now there he is treading his threadbare tires all over that history like it was nothing.

And just like that, while still in state, an idea suddenly pops into Landon's noggin like a revelation from the ethereal realms and the more he thinks about it the more real it becomes, all the little details falling into place like markers on the road. He sees the path wide and clear in front of him and all he needs to do is take it and never look back. He turns the air-conditioning to full blast, trying to cool his brain down from over-drive to a more manageable pace. He could think of only a few other times in his life when he's experienced this type of tunnel vision, where he could clearly see his future, albeit short-term, laid out in front of him with such mathematical precision. The light at the end of the tunnel is his son. Well, Melanie, too, but the two come as a package deal, he reasons, and who could blame him. But Landon tries hard not to get ahead of himself for once. After all, he has a heist to plan out and execute this afternoon.

* * *

Landon takes a seat in the bleachers at the old Derby Dolls roller rink. About a dozen girls skate around the banked track at great speed, oozing aggression. Landon cringes at the sight of the pivot catching a high elbow and ending up on her lily ass.

"You keep flappin' those wings you gonna fly right the fuck outta here," the coach barks out as he rushes to the railing. Frankie DiDio has carefully cultivated his boot-camp-instructor persona: the buzz cut, the fatigues, the phony appearance of having things firmly under control. It does give him street cred, on sight, and leverage with a certain class of ladies, gluttons for punishment, even when his own conditioning is lacking, and his weight has ballooned for no apparent reason as he's pushing forty with a chronic bad back. He and Landon are army buddies, and that's a bond that cuts through all the mundane bullshit, of which there's been plenty to go around. They pulled all kinds of odd jobs together over the years, working the door at Bo Kaos on the weekends back in the day, then running security detail at various events in Hollywood, or bodyguarding for Armenian and Chinese mobsters, all of which exposed them to a side of the city that only bursts into public consciousness with the occasional bloody headline before quickly receding back into the shadows. They almost came to blows on several occasions, over either pussy or money or simply as victims of self-created Hobbesian traps, but they always ended up burying the hatchet deep in some WeHo dive bar, usually the Frolic Room.

The pivot picks herself up off the floor and rolls back on the track, blonde locks jutting out from under the helmet. Stephanie waves slightly in Landon's direction before switching effortlessly into a killer on wheels. The name on back of her jersey reads *Barbie Drone*.

"I'm gonna get that fuckin bitch," Stephanie, or rather Barbie Drone, proclaims.

"Yeah, please help yourself," Frankie says, stroking the IUD he's wearing like a pendant around his neck. He turns to take his seat back in the first row next to an open bottle of beer when he spots Landon a couple rows back. "Where the fuck you been, man? Thought you was dead."

Landon's head bobs up and down. "Oh, you know me, just trying to keep body and soul together," he says.

He jumps over another row, gets closer to Frankie, and shows him the recoupment letter.

"Did you get one of these?"

"Yeah, got mine couple of days ago. I say we start a war. Right here in Cali," Frankie says.

"Can you drive a truck?" Landon asks.

Frankie jumps out of his seat to bark at a player but pulls his back and freezes before he scats that scream to a whimper. "Yeah, I can drive a truck."

"I don't mean like a U-Haul or a pickup truck. I mean like one of 'em big rigs, eighteen-wheeler fuckers," Landon says.

Frankie holds his back as he sits back down.

"I can drive it forwards, backwards, parallel park it, hotwire it, hell, I can do donuts with the sumabitch. So, yeah, I can drive a truck," he says.

"Where'd you pick that up?" Landon asks.

"Kuwait City," Frankie says, like something got stuck in his throat.

"Oh, before my time," Landon says.

"Naw, you was there," Frankie says. "Holed up in the brig, staying true to your name. It was when we beat up on that ensign, if I recall, scored one for the below-the-deckers."

Landon smiles at the memory. "Oh, yeah, shoulda been you in the brig, I barely scratched the guy."

"We had a shipment of Strykers, had to line-haul 'em into Basra and they were short on drivers, so they trained some of us. Rode the Highway of Death all the way to Hell and back." Landon takes a swig out of Frankie's bottle, his head trying to disconnect from the past. "I was drinking that," Frankie says, before redirecting his anger at the players. "Gimme four laps, fast as you can."

"You can't drink," Landon says. "You'll be driving a truck in a couple hours. I got a solid tip and I thought…" Landon lets that hang for a moment. "Now here's an opportunity, presents itself, right?"

"You talkin' about stealing," Frankie says with the excitement of a child getting the correct answer in grammar school.

"Well, yeah."

"Why would you steal a fuckin' truck?" Frankie asks.

"It's what's *inside* the truck, dummy. *Cigarettes*," Landon says. "We got no choice, Frankie. It's written in the fuckin' stars."

"No shit. Who else is in on it?"

"Just you, me, and a pretty girl." That'd be Stephanie, fresh off the track, casually sliding onto Landon's lap right on cue. She's pretty, in a Suicide Girls kind of way, especially with her derby doll gear on, helmet dangling on her hand like a severed head.

"Hey, where the hell have you been? I was worried about you," Stephanie says.

"I think I slept for like four days straight," Landon says.

"Don't blame you. That was some crazy shit!" she says, eyeing both Landon and Frankie in turns. "Right? Right?" With no apparent invitation, she stands up and lifts her skirt, exposing her right buttock to Landon. "Look, I got a fresh bruise right here." She then grabs Landon's hand and drags him away like a hooker in the lobby of a house of ill repute. She puts her helmet back on because, well, she means business, that's why.

Judging by the way the next episode unfolds, or *doesn't* unfold, depending on perspective, if Stephanie were the paying party she'd be entitled to a refund. She does let out some moans, facing the wall of a dark hallway leading to the locker rooms, but they signal exasperation more than anything, seeing as Landon is fresh out of vital fluids, having just tapped out for his ex not an hour ago. He pulls his pants up and steps away graciously, the least he can do. "Sorry, my mind is elsewhere," he says, his ego in the basement, "but I can eat you out...?" Stephanie takes her helmet off and throws it at him, hitting him squarely in the chest. "I hate hating, but I'm hating on you right now."

Theirs has been a volatile relationship from the beginning. They met at a Halloween Party in Hermosa Beach the year before and instantly connected when they played the old parlor game "Who's your favorite Buddha?" At the count of three they both blurted out "Buddha *Amitabha*!" and then shared a long, warm hug where no words were spoken, or for that matter necessary. Buddha Amitabha's nineteenth vow was to appear before those who called upon him on the moment of death and offer them protection and safe passage to his Paradise of Ultimate Bliss. The idea appealed greatly and equally to Stephanie's New Age hipster friends and Landon's North Long Beach ghetto brothers alike, as it promised safe spiritual refuge after a life lived at one's contentment, a philosophy of life akin to riding a roller-coaster into the Big Nightclub. All they had to do was remember the password to this ultimate VIP lounge. Easier said than done, as Landon found out during his first tour in Iraq when an IED shrapnel pierced his right shoulder and, as he came to, all he could think about was: first, was he still alive? Check, apparently. No limbs missing? Check. Cock and balls still there? Triple check. Repeat. Then for the next hour, as he was being medevacked to Camp Arifjan out in Kuwait, his thoughts revolved mainly around home, what with the rumors of Melanie's infidelity he'd been hearing about through the grapevine. He imagined what impact his death would have on his wife and son Jason (this was before Tyler was born), how they would take the news if he were to die, how they might carry on with their lives without him, how he would be remembered, if at all. Would they bring flowers to his grave? Scratch that, he'd asked to be cremated, his ashes thrown over the 6th Street Bridge for the trains to carry them into the four corners of the earth. Anyway, soon as he came out of surgery the nurse informed him that he would live, the wound would heal, and he'd be back at one hundred percent in just a few short months. Landon was so high on painkillers he vaguely remembered telling the nurse how the French call an orgasm *la petite mort*, the little death, that there's something about death and sex that seem to go hand in hand and seeing that life is so frail would she mind giving him a hand job, for country and flag and all. He also vaguely remembered getting one but for all he knew it might have been self-inflicted. Probably was. Post-surgery all he dreamed about was to leave the theater of war but a.s.a.p. and return home to catch his son Jason's first day of school, a wish he got just a few days later. Actually, Landon believed it in his heart that it was originally *Jason*'s wish and not his, and it was only due to the strong psychic connection that had developed between them that the wish popped into Landon's head in the first place, and in actuality Jason might have been the prime mover to the entire sequence of events leading him back home just in time to save his marriage.

All that to say that not even for a moment throughout this whole ordeal did Landon think even once about Buddha Amitabha. It was only on his flight back home, while gazing out the window at an ephemeral formation of noctilucent clouds, that the thought crossed his mind and he banged his head on the window and reproached himself in silence, even shed a few tears and promised to do better next time, as he understood that he had just been tested.

* * *

The railroad track feeds into the depot terminal and a crane whirrs and screeches as it lifts a trailer off the train car. Landon and Frankie observe the action via binoculars from the comfort of Stephanie's Shelby Mustang convertible, limited edition, a birthday present from her godfather or maybe uncle, Landon isn't quite sure who the donor was or why on earth he'd gift such an extravagant pony car to her. She let him drive it quite often, so he didn't care to ask for details. Like how could she afford a $4500 a month loft in downtown? And why couldn't Landon be at her place between two p.m. and five p.m. on Tuesdays?

They spot Melanie as she walks around the terminal holding a clipboard. A young, burly truck driver puts his greasy signature on the delivery papers. The door to the depot office opens and Landon cringes at the sight. Ray Barba, a middle-aged man dressed sharply in a crisp suit, walks up to his fiancé, Melanie, and the two have a brief chat. Just before they go their separate ways Ray grabs a handful of Melanie's ass. She feigns disapproval but with a smile.

"Ouch!" Frankie says, needing no binoculars to spot the infringement. "That's your ex, innit?" Frankie asks. "Now I get it. Your disappearing act."

"Fuck you guys talking about—" Stephanie says.

The Mack tractor backs up and rams under the marked trailer. It wedges the kingpin locked, and the coupled unit rocks back and forth to secure the lock.

"Damn, this is gettin me horny. That weird?" Stephanie says.

* * *

The speedometer on the Mustang hovers at around forty-five, Stephanie's goldilocks blowing in the wind like flocks out of Medusa's head. A car honks as it passes by her, but she doesn't turn, she just smiles like reading a sign that says the plan is going to work. Her eyes are glued to the Mack truck in the slow lane in front of her. She catches up with it, hooning like crazy, toying with it, just maybe a nose ahead, enough for the truck driver to take notice of her. She casually looks up, as if by accident, and catches the trucker's eye. She smiles, and he grins like an idiot. All she has to do now is reel him in.

Stephanie accelerates ever so slightly and the truck stays with her. She turns and flashes that beautiful Cali smile again. The trucker tips the brim of his greasy hat, like he has a real chance there. She waits until there's eye contact, then points to the back of his truck. The trucker shakes his head, confused. Stephanie flails her arms, signaling that something is wrong with the truck, possibly a flat tire, hard for anyone to understand what she means.

The trucker adjusts his rearview mirror, rolls down the window, but can't quite make out the damage. Stephanie honks a few times to make her point before speeding off into the sunset like a good Samaritan.

Landon, at the wheel of a beat-up Corolla a few car lengths behind, and Frankie, riding shotgun, keep a close tab on the action. Landon slows down and edges into the lane behind the cargo truck. "C'mon, man, pull over," he mumbles. Having crashed on Frankie's couch more times than a cockroach, Landon is familiar with this area of Long Beach, what he calls Baghdad by the Bay, and he knows that once the truck hits the freeway it won't stop until it reaches destination.

Landon keeps his distance until, finally, the truck signals for a turn. It pulls up on the shoulder of the road, close to an overpass, hazard lights blinking. The trucker jumps out and proceeds with a quick inspection. He bops the tires with a mallet, checking for flats. Left side first, then circles around the back. As he does that, Landon pulls up roadside of the truck and Frankie rushes out of the passenger seat and into the truck's cabin fast as a jailbreak.

This is when Landon first notices the strange figure standing tall in the middle of the overpass, looking down on the action. The lanky, swarthy man wears a long, dark overcoat, bowtie and top hat, a strange getup for that neck of the woods and that time of day. Odder yet, he carries with him a suitcase. Not a briefcase, mind you, a *suitcase*. He is, to Landon's mind, some kind of Traveler. But what Landon finds most disturbing is the fact that this mysterious Traveler isn't trying to record or photograph the thieves in flagrante delicto, he isn't there to witness, he is there in *judgment*. Landon has no doubt about that.

Landon helps Frankie up in the cab and to their delight the keys are still in the ignition, as expected. Frankie pushes into the clutch, whacks a red button on the dash and gives Landon the thumbs up as the truck takes off with a whoosh. In the rearview mirror of his own car Landon spots a really animated truckless driver jumping up and down for some reason. "Sucker," he says, but catches his own reflection in the mirror and out of sheer anger he tries to spit out the side window, not realizing it's closed, and his spit splashes all over it like a cracked rotten egg.

Landon looks up to the overpass as he drives through, but the Traveler has already vanished. He spots a rainbow in the horizon, although it hasn't rained in months, the holy fires are raging from Siskiyou County to Shasta to Sylmar, and the bone-dry earth is crying for thunder. He wants to call his buddy for confirmation of what he's just witnessed but the rattle and hum of emerging traffic soon closes in on him like an iron maiden and the moment is gone forever.

* * *

The Sun is visible just above the flat roof of the warehouse, looking west over the 5 Freeway, giving no respite from the heat just yet. Landon expertly flips a jackknife to saw the seal off the back of the trailer. "I've dealt with him before. Guy's fair as a fairy," he says. "He's got like an army of vending machines all over town. He's gonna sell these for top dollar."

"I don't even know what I'm gonna do with all that dough. Did you even think about that?" Frankie says.

"I got debt collectors breathing down my neck. I wanna settle."

"That's just plain stupid, man," Frankie says, insulted to the core. "Not to mention un-American. It's the Life of Riley for *this* motherfucker, I tellya that."

"L.A. or TJ?" Landon asks.

"Tijuana first, then L.A., bro," Frankie says, "you know how that goes."

"I hear ya. Every now and then you gotta balance the books, or someone's gonna do it for you," Landon says. A door opens behind him and out comes Lex 'Tallyanis', a former prize-fight promoter, now in his late fifties, slicked-back hair, short but still trim and fit, got a late line on vending machines when a city route opened for bidding and he made sure his offer was the only one, and here he is five years later with hundreds of these cash cows spread all over town like pockmarks.

Landon makes the introductions, "Frankie, this is Lex Tallyanis. Lex, this is Frankie, guy I told you about."

"You Italian?" Frankie asks, dumbly, yet sincerely. "I heard that correctly?"

Lex ignores him, points to the name painted on the back door. "This one of Ray Barba's trucks, right?"

"I guess so. Difference does it make?" Landon says.

Lex lifts the door open and climbs inside. He takes a boxcutter to the first sealed load resting on a pallet and exposes a row of cigarette cartons.

"We happy?" Landon asks.

"Sure. Why don't you fellas come inside for a minute," Lex says, and Frankie promptly jumps *inside* the truck, looking around like where's the beef. Lex points at the warehouse and addresses Frankie very slowly, as if talking to a child, "Inside *there*."

Landon takes a seat under the air conditioning fan, dreaming about the near future, and smiles. Lex tosses some mini bottles of whiskey in Landon's general direction and plays catch with some mini bags of chips.

"I'm gonna call my cousin to bring the cash over, all right?" Lex says.

"You don't have it on you? I was under the impression you had the dough in the house," Landon says.

"No, where am I gonna keep it here? Damn warehouse. It'll be twenty minutes. You can wait twenty minutes. It's like ten grand a minute, do the math, to sit on your ass, eat chips and drink whiskey," Lex says. "Hey, I'd want that fucking job."

The math goes over Frankie's head like homework, and he gets restless, which in turn makes Landon nervous. "I don't trust this guy," Frankie says, soon as Lex is out of range.

"Got a better idea?"

"The Chinaman," Frankie says.

Landon shudders at the thought. Only as a last resort, if his family's life depended on it, would he ever try to sell to the Chinaman, such is his reputation. According to one such wild rumor, the Chinaman tracked down his estranged brother, who for practical purposes involving organ harvesting was worth more to the Chinaman dead than alive, at a remote retreat near Mt. Baldy. The brother had given himself up to a life of solitary asceticism and was deep in contemplation when our Chinaman appeared one day in front of him carrying his beloved meat cleaver, made of an alloy of steel and meteorite. And at the exact moment the Chinaman brought his meat cleaver down onto his brother's head, the monk's body spontaneously transformed into light. Poof! Just like that, body of light. Rainbow light, to be precise. Which, to Chinaman's chagrin, fared much better against a sharp blade than your common human flesh. Subsequently, the Chinaman banned all rainbow displays in his sight, be they on purpose or by accident, such as reflections on cutlery or windows, and anyone guilty of such was to suffer greatly. His chefs, at a great disadvantage for having to work with greasy sauces and whatnot, were the first to go, and the whole incident just showed to all that the Chinaman really knew no limits. Landon, fair to say, does not see himself as the folk hero to test those limits. So…

Landon has no choice but cool Frankie off with some story about Lex, trying to get Frankie to find comfort in the familiar. He tells him everything is mini with Lex, from his tiny bottles of booze to his tiny boots, except his loyalty to his extended family, so it's no surprise Lex would entrust his cousin with this money. For if the world feels small to Landon, so it does to Lex and his first cousin, once removed, first of their name and the first of their kin to be born in the States, which has made them overly supportive of each other's ambitions and willingness to *make* it, where their elders had in the past been stunted and denied. This drive also explains the cousins' obsession with ostentatious things, like flashy sports cars, bespoke Italian suits, or front row season tickets to the Lakers. And while this backstory has sprung out of Landon's imagination, he knows it's not entirely out of whole cloth, but rather something put hastily together out of found parts. In any case, it does the trick, as Frankie fakes a yawn and says, "Cool story, bro."

Landon checks his watch, an hour has gone by and still no cash. In the meantime, Lex has joined them back inside and Landon is telling him how he and Frankie became friends. "We were having this highfalutin discussion about the nature of God and the Universe, and he was just sitting there quietly all this time, when all of a sudden he blurts out, 'I only think of God when I get an erection!' I swear to god, maybe I'm a complete idiot, but out of that whole fuckin' conversation that's the only thing I remember."

Lex pulls the brakes on his laugh soon as it gets out. "Well, *are* you?"

Landon quickly rolls back his laughter. "What's that?"

"Are you an *idiot*?" Lex deadpans.

Landon glances at Frankie, as the temperature in the room suddenly drops to a freeze. Lex casually checks his cell phone, like they're talking about the weather or something.

"No, I'm not an idiot. I'm just a misfit," Landon says, and looks at Frankie for support but can't read much into one raised eyebrow.

"How's that?" Lex asks.

"Can't quite fit the things I done wrong with the punishment I been given," Landon says, quoting from a book he's once read and long forgotten.

"It all evens out in the end, don't it," Lex says.

"End of *what*?"

They all turn at the same time as the doors hurl open like the gates of hell welcoming Attila the Hun. Ray and two goons, built like twin Kenmore refrigerators, flash their handguns to signal their intent, old-school like. Landon gets up, his mind churning through the options.

"Don't make me chase you down now, Landon," Ray says, then proceeds to make the proper introductions, just so everyone is clear on who to kill first if the shit hits the fan. Turns out, Ray Barba is the cousin Lex spoke of. Landon feels like a complete idiot, staring at a simple puzzle an ape would've solved in under a minute. He knows similar things of both Lex and Ray, like the front-row Lakers season tickets, the sob stories of their immigrant families hailing from the same corner of the world, same tailored suits, and so forth. For Chrissakes, they even look alike with their hangdog faces if you squint a little. Landon knows that when this small world puts two and two together for you, you're at the Fates' mercy. The goons circle around the table. They frisk Landon first, then Frankie, on which they find a small arsenal. While the goons are busy collecting the weapons, keys, wallets, condoms, and other such *objets de vertu*, Ray launches into an ad hoc speech that he's probably rehearsed on the way over in front of a pocket mirror. He takes a seat on the edge of the table, eyes still locked on Landon, his chest puffing. "You tell me, Landon, what makes a man, with a capital M? Is he a Man who's in the world but not *of* this world, a man who thinks and talks but can't provide for his family, is he a Man?" At about this point Landon more or less checks out, realizing Ray was trying to make himself look like Henry V in front of his goons. The rest of his speech goes something along the lines of, hey, the world is rotten, everyone's crooked, and if you know the rules of the game you play it to its limits, while the lesser men (e.g. Landon) are just sitting in the nosebleeds bitching about the no-calls, all this registering to Landon as *blah blah blah*.

"So, did you get the invitation to our wedding?" Ray asks, as a way to bring his motivational speech to an end, a question that comes out of left field for Landon, but then so did Ray.

"Not formally," Landon says.

"I'd really like it for you to be there. So let me know," Ray says and turns to face the rest of the audience, "His ex-wife will soon be *my* wife. Everybody wins."

Ray takes out a card and places it on the table in front of Landon. "I think it'd be good for your kid, too. Don't wanna be a total stranger. Other day I took him to one of 'em pony rides up there at—"

"Griffith Park," Lex chimes in.

"At Griffith Park. They got these mini horses, swear to god, they're cute as fuck. Cute-as-fuck. With the long hair and the little boots. Clackity-clack-clackity."

"Hooves," Lex says.

"Kid ate it up, he loves horses. End of the day he says to me, get ready for this, says to me, quote, 'This was the most fun I ever had. Ever-ever.' Unquote. Ain't that sumthin, huh? More like a dad to him than you ever been. And it's on account of kiddo and Melanie that you're not already dead," Ray says, nodding with gravity to the lesser man, "He had another son, but he died a couple years back. Wanna tell 'em what you were doing when that happened, Landon? Picking up your Father of the Year trophy?"

"You don't know shit, asshole!" Landon says. He means to say more but the words get stuck in his throat. He could never explain to someone what happened that night. Who'd understand? Frankie? Stephanie? Tyler? *Melanie*? Nah, especially her. He can't believe she spilled the beans to this fuckin' poseur. The little she knew. So he simply shuts down whenever the subject comes up.

"Take it easy on him, Ray," Lex says.

"Pardon me?"

"Well, he's dumbed down in the name of love, not for worldly gains. I can appreciate the difference, such as it is," Lex says.

"Either way it's an act of aggression. Is it not?" Ray says. The goons nod. "As such, it needs to be punished."

"Guy just flipped you the birdie, Ray. Metaphorically speaking, of course," Lex says. "You got your truck back, punishment should fit the crime."

Ray takes his coat off and leans into Landon, close enough to hear his heartbeat. "So what's it gonna be?"

"That's a good question, Ray," Landon says. Ray taps on the wedding invitation. "The wedding, dipshit. You comin'?"

"I wouldn't miss it for the world," Landon says.

Ray sticks his hand out for a shake and Landon reciprocates with a limp hand. "Get up, the both of you," Ray orders them.

Landon gets up slowly, his chair squeaking against the floor. He looks down at Frankie, who hasn't budged. He thinks Frankie must have spaced out for a moment, and he's about to nudge him into action, when—

"Are you bitches gonna pay us our money now… or *what*?" Frankie belts out and slams his hand hard on the table. He then cracks his knuckles and glances at his buddy, and Landon instantly knows what he means. Frankie is recalling his brief flirtation with a Communist party cell and his subsequent work for a truckers' union, a job that ended prematurely when a considerable amount of cash, to the tune of twenty thousand, went missing from Frankie's ledgers, an incident for which he pleaded the fourth *and* the fifth and surprisingly got away with only a few broken bones, which only proved to him that the money had been stolen so many times over that it had no rightful owner.

Frankie's just signaled to Landon that he misses his union issue brass knuckles but, just the same, wastes no time punching one of the goons hard in the balls. He yanks Ray aside, ripping his crisp designer suit like a used ticket, then elbows the other goon in the jaw and it looks for a brief moment like he's gonna tear through the remainder of the room in no time, when a shot rings out fit to stop anyone in his tracks. This gets Frankie's attention all right. Ray stands there with his gun pointed at him while the goons pick themselves off the floor.

"Hands down on the table," Ray says, as he removes his tattered blazer. Soon as Landon complies he swiftly grabs his middle finger and snaps it back hard as he can. The bones crack like twigs. Landon howls. He flails wildly in his chair, a goon having a tough time restraining him.

"Does the punishment fit the crime now, Lex?" Ray asks.

There's a moment of dreaded silence, a goon's gun pointed at Frankie's head. Ray feigns a punch, but Frankie doesn't flinch. "What's your jerkoff hand, tough guy?" Ray asks. Frankie glances to his left hand, then his right hand. "That a trick question, motherfucker?" Frankie asks.

* * *

The door blasts open as the goons unceremoniously hurl Landon and Frankie out the door, Landon holding his right hand in pain, Frankie his left. Ray follows them out and watches them scurry away until they disappear behind the warehouse.

"We gotta get us a medic," Frankie growls.

"Fuck is wrong with you, man. Why did you have to go off on them like that?" Landon says.

"I don't know, bro. My brain told me to follow my instincts. It just felt like the right thing to do at the time," Frankie says.

Landon stops, peeks back around the corner and in the direction of the truck. "No cash, no credit cards, no phones, looks like a long walk to the hospital," he says. "Say, you still got that pocketknife?"

Frankie reaches down into his boots. "Yeah, what about it?"

Landon heads straight to Ray's Cadillac Escalade and sticks the pocketknife into its tires. God, he hates that motherfucker and the car he rode in on. He then does the same to the rest of the handful of cars parked in the lot. The air hisses out of the tires as they go flat. Frankie crouches down next to Landon.

"Okay, so now *they* can't leave either. That the idea?" Frankie asks. "Brilliant." They sneak back behind the cigarette truck. "Earlier, when I asked you if you can drive a truck, what did you say?" Landon asks.

"I said, yes. I lie to you?" Frankie says and puts his left hand up like he's about to swear with crossed fingers on a stack of Bibles, a move just fast enough to send his broken middle finger flapping out of view.

"You said you could drive it, you could do donuts with it, you said you could hot-wire it—," Landon says.

"You bet, man," Frankie says.

Landon points up to the open window on the driver side of the truck. "We're *driving* the fuckin' truck outta here."

Landon and Frankie labor down in the gutter of the cabin, using their good hands until they free up some wires. Judging by the groans it's just as hard as it looks. "My fuckin' back!" Frankie cries out as his body jolts, and he bangs his head on the underside of the dashboard. Somehow the wires cross to start the engine and the truck roars to life.

Frankie struggles with the steering wheel, using his right arm going round and round. Landon helps out with his one good hand, the two looking like Siamese twins trying to slip out of a straitjacket. Landon looks in the side rear-view mirror. Ray and his panicked goons rush out of the warehouse and scramble to their car. Landon sounds the warning, "They're coming!"

"Yeah, good luck with that," Frankie says, and he blares the horn a few times to let them know who's in charge.

* * *

They have just hit the 405-N when Landon, who has been unusually quiet for an adrenaline junkie, slams the dashboard in anger. "Goddammit, man! Goddammit!!"

"What's the problem? You in shock?" Frankie asks.

Landon holds his broken finger up. "That's my pussy finger, man."

"Damn. Sorry, bro." Frankie says with a rare show of empathy, as he changes lanes, shaking his head at his friend's misfortune. Landon stares out the window, inconsolable. "You realize, we just done start a war," Frankie notes, in passing. "Fuckin love it, man."

"How do you see this ending?"

"Can't worry about that… like you said, it's already written in the stars, innit?"

The truck changes lanes to overtake a slow-moving bus. It swishes gently and Landon notices for the first time a moving object in the middle of the bus's dashboard. It keeps shaking its head, a dashboard bobblehead Buddha swaying with the turns in the road. And not just any Buddha, it dawns on Landon, but Buddha *Amitabha*.

"Frankie—"

"Yeah."

"You ever think of dying?" Landon asks.

"Nope. You?"

"It's a funny thing, y'know. Much as I try I just can't picture myself dead. Why do you think that is?"

Landon asks, as he glances over at his buddy to demand an answer, but none is forthcoming.

An earthquake expert on the AM radio station rings the alarm bells for the imminent Big One, being not a matter of if but *when*. Landon turns the radio off and eases his mind into the hum of the West-bound traffic, which presently comes to a halt and as he looks at the road ahead to see a mile-long snake of cars heading mercilessly into the mouth of the sinking Sun, for one brief moment he feels at peace with the world.

They spend the rest of the ride in funereal silence.

*"Do not take pleasure
 in the soft smoky light
of the hell dwellers."*

The Tibetan Book of the Dead, Day Two

The long hours spent at the West Anaheim Medical Center have only helped to exacerbate Landon's sense of entrapment into a world that offers no possibility of an honorable discharge, or none that he could see. Something about hospitals in general makes him feel ill at ease even when he's just visiting, let alone as a patient, and he's always held a secret wish that he would much rather suffer a sudden and violent death than go through a protracted terminal illness that would confine him to such a sterile and alien environment. He sees the latter option as too much of a burden on the soul. He could take the physical pain but, by god, let that be in a place that stimulates the senses if nothing else.

Through the small window in the door to his ward he can see a large gathering of people, about twenty strong, waiting impatiently in the lobby, most of them sharing similar features, big round eyes and angular jaws like he's seen in some old photographs of Ellis Island emigrants, telling Landon they were all of a kin, there to watch over the fate of a loved one. Later on, he manages to sneak a peek in the adjacent room and spots there a little girl, can't be more than a year old, tubes running out of her body making her look like a tiny spider, a man and a woman praying silently at her bedside. They're holding hands, the couple, heads resting on each other, looking almost like they're praying not only for the health of their child but for themselves to survive the heavy blow lurking around the corner.

Landon wonders if the child's fate is already sealed by some divine judgment whose implications are too obtuse for anyone to fully comprehend without the benefit of life-long hindsight, or do those prayers carry enough weight to tip the balance in favor of life. It seems to Landon that, paradoxically, the scale would side with Life only if Death itself were thrown in. As the answer to that question becomes clear in his mind he finds that the only way to articulate it is to walk straight to the lobby, nudge his way into the circle of praying uncles and aunts, and proceed to throw his lot in by singing a Buddhist mantra while everyone stops and wonders who the hell this strange man is.

Om Mani Padme Hum. Om Mani Padme Hum.

* * *

Upon learning of his father's cancer Landon tried to understand the mystery of that nasty disease. He didn't go about looking for a cure, but he pictured himself in his dad's shoes and imagined what that'd be like, how he would deal with that cruel knock on fate's door. It was just a simulation game, but he reckoned he'd just blow his brains out before letting the chemo poisons take their toll. He shuddered at the thought of losing all his hair, which he made a point out of not cutting after coming back home from his last deployment, his mane now stylishly hanging in a ponytail good to give Samson a run for his money. He would sometimes even style it in a man bun on top of his head, like in the sculptures he'd seen of the Scythian sage, though that look would instantly label him, in the eyes of many, as some kind of nonchalant boho, one more parasite the genteel society has to tolerate. Not that Landon gives two shits about that, goes without saying.

He once opened a book at random, which was his way of divination, a kind of *sortes sanctorum* for the hoi polloi, and came across an exchange between Socrates and his disciples, the wise man decrying the Greek physicians' approach to illness as being limited to the ailing part of the human body. But Socrates, who was no fool and had been schooled in the nature of various maladies by a Thracian physician of the god-king Zalmoxis, begged to differ. The gist of it was you can't treat the eyes without the head, can't treat the head without the body and, likewise, you can't treat the body without the soul, for all that is good or bad in the body flows from the soul. This struck Landon as the truth, and he implicitly trusted Socrates upon learning that he'd also served in battle in his youth and Landon imagined a bond between them, like a golden thread spanning centuries. This whole thing got Landon started on his soul work, though he had no idea how to go about it at first and he just spent countless hours listening to soul music, which did little to raise his awareness other than that of the opposite sex.

The attractive resident doctor informs Landon of the Bennet's fracture in his right middle finger and the irony is not lost on him when she tries to set his bones straight by using a Chinese trap, a deceptively benign contraption that only tightens around his finger the more he pulls. "This fuckin' thing reminds me of my ex-wife," Landon says, but the doctor doesn't find it amusing. "She was very possessive, is what I mean," he says, trying to score some cheap points on the rebound, failing just the same.

"Do you like your job?" Landon asks.

"I love my job, I've always wanted to be a doctor," she says, and she feeds him some painkillers.

"You should thank me, then," Landon says.

"Why is that?"

"You're a doctor, your job is to nurse people back to health, is it not?"

"Yeah," the doctor says, checking her watch.

"Well, here I am, giving you the *opportunity* to practice what you love," Landon says, and takes a deep breath, feeling some warmth inside already.

"Why, thank you, Landon Briggs," she says, and pats Landon gently on the shoulder, not to goad him on but to settle him in, knowing that the meds would knock him out soon enough.

"A man once told me…" Landon begins his rant, "He was in a wheelchair, this man… Been like that all his life… polio or something… can't recall… had a smile on his face like a double fucking rainbow, even when it rained… especially when it rained… and me, in my prime, walking around like the sky was falling… not to mention good looking, ha-ha... I asked him why he seemed so happy all the time... he said to me, he said... I *chose* this life... I asked, what do you mean... you're in a goddamn wheelchair... He said he saw it in a dream, saw himself before coming down into this world, into that sick body... he made a *choice* to live that life... so that other people can have the experience to care for him... if not for the sick, the maimed, the crippled... who would you look after... You understand now... Be thankful for people like me... I *chose* to come down here with this broken finger... you better believe it... I chose *you*, gorgeous..."

The local anesthetic kicks in and Landon wills it to wash over his entire body like a self-induced ritual cleansing and before long all that clatter in his head, all his current concerns about his life, his son's future, the state of his broken pussy-finger, or the fate of the stolen truck, it all subsides to a humming didgeridoo drone and then he's out like a light.

* * *

Landon is still running on Novocain fumes when he finds himself on his way to a Halloween party at a Torrance funeral house just after midnight. A friend of a friend of Stephanie's knows some guy, Cassidy, a sourpuss who runs a truck repair shop and he's supposed to be at this party. Stephanie's idea is to try to talk Cassidy into taking the stolen truck in for a few days under the false pretense of repairing it, and so hide it before it gets discovered, parked as it currently is across nine parking spots behind the loading dock of a CVS pharmacy. What they call a long shot. Landon slouches into his seat, turns the heat on and angles the air vents upward to let the warm draft blow over his face. He then closes his eyes, like hanging a do-not-disturb sign on a hotel door.

"I had a bad feeling about yesterday. I've been having these recurrent nightmares. It's like my Barbies are turning into vampire snakes or basilisks or some kind of monsters. I feel like the Universe is trying to send me a message," Stephanie says, as they hit the freeway.

She nudges Landon, "Are you listening to what I'm saying?" but it's clear that he's either fast asleep or pretending to be. Frankie, on the other hand, is getting a second wind and lending a friendly ear to Stephanie is in fact no problem at all. "I think it could be a metaphor, y'know, for... *consumerism*," Frankie says, nodding like he's half expecting someone in an official capacity to pop out of nowhere and hang a medal on his neck for the brilliance of his comment.

Stephanie signals left, slides effortlessly into the carpool lane, then looks at Frankie in the rearview mirror as if seeing him for the first time. "That's just about the dumbest thing I ever heard," she says. "I mean it, Frankie."

"Well, c'mon now," Frankie says, not one to get easily discouraged by mere words. "If you ever wanna talk about it…" and he gently touches her right shoulder in a gesture of reconciliation and maybe a prelude to something else.

Stephanie acknowledges the overture and pats his hand like you would a child learning his ABC's, but Frankie doesn't seem to mind and nods with all the empathy he could muster after a sleepless and painful night. "And maybe one of these days you can tell me what the fuck a basilisk is," Frankie says.

They pull up into a crowded parking lot that looks like a throwback to an eighties Goth rock music video. Stephanie rubs Landon's shoulder, as to wake him up. "Feeling better?" she asks.

"Wait till I get the hospital bill," he says as he crawls out of the car.

"Bill by bill is how they build the wall, man, between us and them. Hope they take payment in cigarette cartons," Frankie says. "Those motherfuckers." He laughs heartily seeing as he managed to get a chuckle out of Stephanie, which is a victory in itself.

There are caskets everywhere and when Landon first walks in he feels like he's stepped into some Hollywood set decorator's wet dream of a Halloween party. He just wants to find a seat and nod off, but chairs seem to be in short supply, so he lies down on a casket and turns in for the night. A nudge wakes Landon out of his death sleep and he rolls off the casket to a gaggle of laughter. Stevie, the guy who has the run of the place, hovers over him with a shit-eating grin. Stevie casually opens the lid to the casket and Landon realizes that the timber box he's used as a bed isn't there just for show, but it contains an actual corpse.

Landon can't quite pinpoint right away what it is that bothers him about the whole situation. It's not the sight of a dead man, he's seen plenty of dead in his day, and it isn't even the bad form Stevie's shown by flashing the body off like a collector's item to impress a girl. As Landon tries hard to remember why he's at this party in the first place, he bends over and, to everyone's shock, pukes inside the open casket. Now he knows! It's the gaudy make-up on the corpse that's induced in Landon an instant revulsion. It's the thought that the dead man has been stripped of all his dignity and lies there helpless looking as if a blind monkey has used his face to test out a set of liquid lipstick and, when all is said and done, not even God himself could pick him out of a line-up.

Stevie wastes no time poking fun at Landon, calls him a wuss, a cuck, or a bitch, or something to that effect, and the girl beside him laughs heartily with a pitch so high Landon has to cover his ears for fear of having his eardrums blown out. Landon wipes the vomit off his chin then throws a newbie southpaw roundhouse at Stevie but misses and hits the girl square on the jaw and knocks her out for some time. He can't help but wonder, in mid-brawl, if by some subconscious mechanism, or divine justice, the punch originally meant for Stevie ended up with the girl instead. No matter, Stevie grabs him by the collar and headbutts him so hard blood starts gushing down his face like someone has turned on a faucet. The next couple of minutes are a complete blank for Landon but when he finally comes to he sees a big dude putting the hurt on Stevie. A couple of caskets are overturned, lids cracked, make-up stains everywhere. A girl dressed up as Elvira jumps on the big dude's back, but he flicks her aside like a bug. She goes flying and doesn't stop for a second until her face makes a good impression on the wall. Landon looks around at the flat bodies strewn on the floor, can't tell who's dead or who is merely unconscious. He can't tell how long he's been out or how the hell everything's escalated so quickly.

The big dude finally lets Stevie's body drop on the floor like a wet towel, then walks up to Landon and tells him in a strong Eastern European accent, "We better get the fuck out before they kill us and turn us into pretty dolls."

"Thanks for sticking up for me, man," Landon says. "Damn right, pretty dolls."

They weave through the crowd, not quite at full speed, trying to make it look natural and Landon picks up some compliments along the way, a girl saying, "That's rad, man, who're you supposed to be, Chuck Liddell?" then she laughs stupidly, hi-hi, but Landon is too focused on his getaway to care about any of that, let alone get her phone number, which he normally would feel obliged to. He scans the crowd for Frankie and Stephanie but can't spot them and the big dude's Jeep Wrangler is already on the move as Landon clings by the open passenger door and hoists himself in. Soon as they clear the parking lot Landon turns around and spots an F-150 hot on their trail. He knows who it is because he can see the two caskets, one white one black, bouncing up and down on the flatbed of the truck like piano keys every time it goes over a speed bump. A shirtless tattooed man sticks halfway out the passenger window of the truck, yelling like a prophet and waving something Landon can't quite see, but a white flag it ain't. They chase at high speed throughout the deserted streets, two cars racing for the prize of vainglory, Landon and his new buddy being able to outmaneuver and avert the raged posse just as they're getting perilously close. They finally manage to lose their tail for a moment, pull up into a dark alley, kill the lights and wait. The crescent moon throws Landon a friendly smile, and they sit there in silence for a full ten minutes, contemplating mortality and gaudy doll-like corpses, until at last they see the brights of the F-150 going the other way, and hear the atavistic guttural shouts of a perturbed man fade in the distance like a wounded coyote cursing the distant highway.

"What's your name, again?" Landon asks.

"Cazimir, but everybody call me Cassidy," the big dude says in the way of introducing himself, like Tarzan. "Everybody know that."

"Landon Briggs," Landon says. "I may have a job for you, Cassidy. There's money."

* * *

Turns out Cassidy indeed runs a truck repair shop in Anaheim and is quite all right with his new best friend forever Landon wheeling the stolen truck in, because what better way to hide something than in plain sight. On one condition. This on account of the strange ways Cassidy goes about his life, like a man walking around with a compass in his hand at all times, even when going to the bathroom.

Cassidy says, "I hide the truck, no problem. For how long, I cannot tell you, because my son he is asleep now, or he is watching cartoons. He is night owl. But I wake him up early, needs to learn. Is up to him, he decide everything around there, you know."

"How old is your son?" Landon asks.

"I have twin boys, Sal and Val," Cassidy says. "One is ten year old, the other is also ten year old. You can imagine."

"No, I mean the one making the decisions around there, how old is *he*?" Landon asks.

"That's Val, he is ten year old, man. How many times I have to tell you?" Cassidy says. "You drunk,

Landon? Or got hit in the head when you little." He laughs.

That's not the kind of exchange to put a two-bit crook's mind at ease but, it's too late for Landon to rock the boat any further. Or the truck. He figures he'll get his answers when the sun comes up and hopefully he'll have moved the elephant-in-the-room into a less conspicuous spot by then.

Cassidy starts up the truck and listens to the rattle and hum of the engine like a doctor looking for arrythmia. "Needs oil change. Also, filter dirty," he says, "bees and moths caught in filter." Cassidy reaches into his pocket and hands Landon a set of keys. "You drive my car, follow me," Cassidy says.

It's a short drive but Landon can barely keep himself awake and soon as they arrive at the truck shop he tells Cassidy he's gonna take a nap in the truck until the querent, Val or Sal, arrives in the morning. Cassidy promises he won't be long, and it seems to Landon like five seconds have passed by, rather than three hours to the minute, when the sound of knuckles rapping on the side window wakes him up with a start. Cassidy's got his son Val in tow, and he proceeds to explain the nature of the ritual they're about to perform. It sounds like kooky talk to Landon, and he files this info into a still-awake chamber of his mind with the intent to give it the benefit of the doubt and reassess it later. The boy oracle whispers something to his dad in a strange tongue and Cassidy nods. "It is undecided," Cassidy says to

Landon, "like split decision. You come back in couple days, final verdict."

"I come back in a couple of days," Landon says.

"I will do job on this truck, you will like. I will make truck invisible. Like magic. Poof!" Cassidy says.

Landon makes no mention to Cassidy of what's inside the truck and Cassidy never asks, which suits Landon just fine. There's some concern that Cassidy might open the truck out of curiosity or, more likely, prompted by his ten-year old son and diviner, but Landon is willing to take the risk because, frankly, he has no choice in the matter. Besides, his broken finger is sending waves of pain into his body, and he needs to get home at last.

* * *

The sun is just coming up over the murky Los Angeles skyline and the air is still chilly like last night's afterthought. Landon asks the cab driver to roll up the window — he doesn't get why these cabbies always have their windows open, maybe to blow away the stench of a busy night ferrying the lowlifes from station to station — and the driver begrudgingly obliges. They drive silently through the awakening giant of a city. Light reflects in Landon's sunglasses, bright, dim, wavy rainbows, flares, a light show of sorts, colors he is sure he hasn't seen before, and he squints every now and then, as if to tell the Sun itself to take it easy on him, but It won't listen.

Landon revels in that state of wakefulness, caught as he is between full awareness and sleep, a state of in-between, an island where the rules of this world are bent or worse, and yet he could always find there a meaningful image or sound, a metaphysical artifact that, once brought into the real world, named real only by way of convenience, would suddenly reveal itself to be something entirely different, depending on when and where Landon managed to conjure it out of the deep recesses of his mind and use it much like a key to unlock the gates to a larger city, larger even than Los Angeles, larger than the desert, larger than the mind of a bedridden child.

Landon yelps like a hurt puppy when his head bobbles forward as the car comes to a stop in front of his apartment building on Romaine and Fairfax, and he wipes the drool off his chin. Time feels elastic to him, now stretching now contracting. He feels like he's dozed off for hours, but it's only been twenty minutes tops. Weird.

* * *

Landon stops for a moment to admire the late blooming jacaranda trees second-drafting a cross-street, their flowers cascading over the sidewalks and orange pumpkin patches like lazy purple archways and their scent triggering in Landon memories of childhood, of days at the beach and pink dappled sunsets and late-night barbeques imbued with the music of Sublime or The Red Hot Chili Peppers and above all that unique Cali insouciance, and so forever linked in his mind to home. He takes a deep breath and is about to unlock the door to his walk-up rent-control apartment when he notices a dent in the jamb, suspiciously close to the lock, and his senses immediately trigger a state of high alert.

Landon lets the screen door close with its usual squeak and then positions himself with his back flush against the wall, out of the door viewer's range. He hears feet shuffling inside and presently the door cracks open. Landon hurls his body against the door and knocks down the intruder. Predictably, it's one of Ray's goons. Landon rushes inside and looks past the fallen to notice the TV's on a freeze-frame of Sally, the skeletal rag doll from "The Nightmare Before Christmas" and he quickly spots a bottle of lubricant (*his!*) on the coffee table. "Fuckin' freak!" Landon says and kicks the goon in the groin.

Landon moves past stacks of books lying on the floor, past an old guitar with a yellow "Police Line Do Not Cross" strap, and to the closet. He reaches behind a stack of shirts and pulls out a small roll of cash, which he pockets. That's his End of the World cash reserve, to use in case of a complete breakdown of computer networks, a time when credit cards would be as useful as toilet paper, a situation, Landon imagines, much like in the moments following the *Big One*.

And right on cue the building starts to rattle. Strangely, Landon is momentarily proud of himself that, for once, he's prepared for the worst but, alas, this quake isn't quite the Big One, doesn't exactly look like the building's about to slide down the block all of a sudden and get into the carpool lane on the 101 freeway. Still, never a good time for an earthquake. Landon finds it hard to get to the front door, dodging books flying off the shelves and stepping around the shards of glass on the floor.

He just can't believe the bad luck that came his way. In a previous life he must've kicked an orphan in the teeth.

The goon comes to as if Nature itself has grabbed him by the throat. He looks up just as Landon is trying to step over him. He kicks Landon hard in the shins, knocking him back into a wall. Landon gropes for the handle of a baseball bat lying in the debris. He takes a swing at the goon, but the floor moves with another wave of tremors and he misses his target. He does hit the floor though, hard to miss that, and the bat rattles his arm like a tuning fork, calibrating him to the pitch of a viola's first string. He drops the bat and holds his hand in agony.

The goon sees this as an opening but as he prepares his knockout punch a bookcase liberates the wall behind him and comes crashing down on his head.

Landon steps around the carrion and runs for the hills.

He just can't believe the good luck that came his way. In a previous life he must've rescued a monk from a burning temple.

* * *

It's later in the day, on the subway platform at Hollywood and Vine, when Landon sees the Traveler again. He's sitting on a bench, top hat on, suitcase by his side, copy of The Los Angeles Times open in front of him, looking no different than a traveling salesman from the '50s perhaps. He puts the paper down and turns his head as Landon comes down the stairs. Landon's immediate reaction is to pivot around and head for the opposite end of the platform. His heart is beating out of his chest at the thought of the unlikely encounter. Goddamn, this guy is good. This couldn't belong to the realm of sheer coincidence.

The shrill of the incoming train, albeit one going in the opposite direction, is music to Landon's ears.

He waits until the last moment before jumping into the last car, just as the doors are closing shut. He takes a seat by the window and, feeling safe now, he scans the crowd for the Traveler. Sure enough, he's still there on the platform, still as a statue, but he suddenly bolts up and makes a few long strides toward the train, looking like he's going to walk right through it, his unblinking eyes eerily fixated on Landon. Landon flinches as if an invisible hand has just slapped him across the face. God, what a fucking spook!

Landon is now certain he is being followed. But by whom, and for what reason, *that* he couldn't even guess. He does owe money to some shady characters, but this is not the way those fellas go about collecting the debt. There's no finesse to their operations, no subtle games being played there, no gumshoe shadowing you for days. So, okay, Landon reasons, it has to be a debt of some kind, otherwise no one would be interested in him. He first thinks of the money he owes back to Uncle Sam, but this is way too soon, he has at least a couple months before government collectors start pestering him. Maybe it's Debt in a general sense, not necessarily money, but currency of some type. Could be an affair he once had, now a man wants retribution, give Landon a beating in return for loss of face. But why go through all that trouble? He just couldn't wrap his head around that. One thing is certain, the Traveler is not after him to hand him prize money.

Landon initially had no intention of going downtown, but if that's how things panned out so be it. He needs time to process the latest drama and the subway provides the perfect environment for contemplation, like a sensory deprivation room corrupted only by the rhythmic sway and rattle of the train speeding down the slick tracks.

The subway comes to a screeching stop at Vermont/Sunset, where a scraggly old bum gets on the train.

Landon spots the creature at the edge of his peripheral vision and prays to all the gods, kings, and holy ghosts that the bum finds a seat at the opposite end of the near-empty car. The bum has other ideas. He takes a shine to the seat right next to Landon's and that's where he decides to build his nest. He has his headphones on, quietly humming a song.

Landon shifts slightly away, in visible discomfort at the stinking wretch, but doesn't change seats. Sure, he'd arrived there first and planted his flag and pissed around it (not literally, he just had a look in his eyes that produced that effect) to let the other hound dogs know not to fuck with his turf, but this is a different kind of situation.

Landon is reminded of the time, about a year after the death of their first son, Jason, when Melanie offended Heaven itself by unceremoniously and unjustly kicking him out of the house. How he suffered at not being able to see Tyler, his last scion and comfort in this world, how he stalked the school at dismissal time to get a glimpse of his younger son, hoping that one day a nanny would pick him up so he could pretend to accidentally run into them down the street and have a brief moment with him. He roamed the streets at night in a drunken stupor, crashing on friends' couches, not knowing where he was half the time.

One day he spotted Tyler through the school gate, still waiting there to get picked up ten minutes past dismissal, and he worked up the courage to walk up to him. He kissed his boy and barely said a word to him when his teacher approached like a shadow, wanting to ask something or other but being instantly repulsed by Landon's smell, not to mention his man bun. She made a face and pinched her nose and spun around like a cadet, to the amusement of the other parents, who started laughing and talking at Landon's expense. Landon quietly cursed her inability to understand what he was going through and vowed to never be that vile person to openly offend someone, like them or not. He generally stuck by that rule, as he did by another rule that said that if a rule is too strict it ceases to be true. He found that to be true, generally speaking.

As if hearing Landon's thoughts, the wretch turns to him and flashes a toothless smile. Landon nods back at him to acknowledge the receipt of a generous gift.

Fellow travelers all the way to Pershing Square.

* * *

By confiscating his cell phone, wallet, and credit cards, Ray Barba has thrown Landon straight to the Stone Age, needing to resort to payphones for communication. On his scenic ride to the racetrack Landon stops at a 7-11 convenience store and picks up some chewing gum, which entitles him to ask the clerk for some quarters in change, which he'd need to feed the payphone later. The clerk's name badge says 'Bahjat', same name and appearance as an Iraqi translator Landon met during his deployment. Landon's intuition tells him he's an Iraqi refugee, having been allowed in the country after providing services for the American troops. But he looks lost here and despondent, probably working to bring his family over but falling behind in debt. Landon points at his name badge, "Iraq?"

"Yessir, Iraq. You were there, sir?"

Landon wonders what pleasant thing could come out of this conversation, trying as he is to keep Death at bay. "No," he answers. Just the same, Bahjat proceeds to tell Landon about his troubles. He's an engineer by trade, but the federal assistance has run out and no one would hire him, except for menial jobs. He has no friends, he misses his son back in the old country, and on and on he goes, voice cracking, waterworks, etc. Landon tries to give him twenty dollars, but the clerk won't accept it. He doesn't want handouts, he says, he's just glad to see a friendly face.

"Is there a payphone around here?" Landon asks.

"Yes, around the corner, sir, you go out that way and then you turn this way. You cannot miss it," the clerk says. "We sell sanitizer wipes, too."

"What's that?"

"Sanitizer wipes, they are one ninety-nine," the clerk says, holding one such pack at the ready.

It dawns on Landon that using a payphone would first require some sanitary procedure. "Oh, I see. I guess I could use some, huh."

Landon takes his time peeling off the cash with one useful hand. He looks up to the TV screen behind the clerk, showing the morning news. It looks like some tabby cat got stuck in a tree, *again*. "Did they lead with the quake?" Landon asks.

"I beg your pardon?"

Landon points to the TV, "The News, did they show the damage?" The clerk spins around to take a look but all he sees is that damn tabby cat. "What made this damage, sir?"

"The earthquake, of course," Landon says.

"There was an earthquake?" the clerk asks.

"Yes, this morning."

"Today."

"Today. This morning. That's what I'm talking about," Landon says, slightly raising his voice with excitement.

"I see," the clerk mutters, mostly to himself, not doubt pegging Landon for just another cuckoo, an Iraqi vet probably.

"They say how strong it was?" Landon asks.

"What?"

"The earthquake this morning. What do you think I'm talking about?" Landon asks, his frustration building up to a boiling point.

"I don't know, sir. I just got here," the clerk says.

* * *

Landon scrubs the payphone clean with a wipe before dialing the number, all the while holding the receiver a clear two inches away from any orifice, shouting into it like he was holding a bullhorn. "Hey Frankie, they've already been to my place, one of Ray's goons was there… inside my fucking apartment, you believe that?" Landon says into the phone, slowly enunciating each word.

"Did you tell him we ain't ready to negotiate just yet? That we've got a few offers on the table, a goddam bidding war." Frankie says.

"That's not what he was after," Landon says.

"What did he want then?" Frankie asks.

"I'm pretty sure he wanted to kill me," Landon says.

"He wanted *what*? Say again, you sound like you're calling from a tunnel," Frankie says.

"He came to *kill* me," Landon screams, and quickly checks himself as a couple of college girls passing by, letterman hoodies and all, scurry off to a safe space.

"Oh, that's just not cool, man," Frankie says. "He try to shoot you, or how'd he go about it?"

"He tried everything, but I got the better of him. I got lucky with that temblor," Landon says.

"Better be lucky than good, huh."

"What I'm trying to tell you, he's got your wallet, now he knows where you live so it's just a matter of time before they come a-knocking," Landon says, and reluctantly presses the receiver to his ear to better hear the words coming out of Frankie's mouth.

"It don't make sense, they kill us both, they ain't gonna find the truck," Frankie says. "Right?"

"Where are you right now?" Landon asks.

"Maybe kill one of us, torture the other. More like it."

"Where?"

"Where would they torture us? Fuck would I know," Frankie says.

"I asked, where are you right now?"

"Oh, I'm at Steph's. Yeah."

"Oh," Landon says, as the thought grabs hold of him like an electrical current.

"Just came up for a coffee... She offered," Frankie says.

Landon fidgets with the phone, contemplating possibilities. "Yeah?"

"Was on my way out to check up on the truck," Frankie says, "but now I'm thinking—"

"What?" Landon asks.

"Better stay put for a couple hours, what do you think? They don't know where *she* lives," Frankie says.

"Probably a good idea," Landon says, "There's a coffee shop down the block there..."

"I already had coffee," Frankie says.

"I moved the truck anyway," Landon says. "Long story."

"You wanna move the truck?" Frankie screams.

"Meet me at the racetrack, I'll catch you up," Landon says.

"Sorry, I'm losing you... Bad connection, man, where the hell are you calling from? Sounds like you in a tunnel."

"Arcadia," Landon says.

"Move the truck to Arcadia? Fuck's in Arcadia?"

"*I'm* in Arcadia," Landon says, and slams the phone hard in its hook. "Motherfucker."

* * *

Landon asks the cab driver to drop him off close to the Santa Anita racetrack and, as he has an hour to burn, he decides to walk around the city of Arcadia. On the side of an overpass he notes the work of a clever graffiti artist. It depicts four figures, three men and a woman, gathered around a marble casket, one of the men pointing to the words engraved on the stone. It reads 'Egoless in Arcadia.' Landon immediately recalls seeing a painting like that in a coffee table art book at Stephanie's, but can't remember the name of the artist or, for that matter, exactly what the inscription said, or what it meant in plain English. Apparently, Arcadia was a mythical paradisiacal land in ancient mythology, and it strikes him then that the Santa Anita racetrack also resides, with cosmic irony, in a city named Arcadia, which is nobody's idea of Paradise on earth, though not exactly a shithole either. Someone's inside joke, perhaps, but Landon believes there's no such thing as coincidence.

As he steps inside the racetrack he can see the cosmic signs flashing like a fucking lighthouse.

* * *

Landon approaches a wooden railing at the paddocks and leans on it, the morning mist making the air heavy with familiar sounds, smells and regrets. The thoroughbreds are in the process of being schooled, pre-race, an outrider riding alongside the racehorse. Landon waves at one such pair coming down the track, huffing and puffing. The jockey's his old acquaintance, Big Ben, while the outrider is Maya, an attractive young woman with a gentle look in her eyes.

"Hey, Big Ben, when the gates open do the horses *know* they're in a race?" Landon asks.

"Get lost, Landon," Big Ben says.

All right.

The early morning crowd is sparse, a couple of self-service machines in use. Landon has already staked out a place in line, waiting for a booth to open, checking his betting card one more time, mouthing Roger Wilco into an invisible microphone linking up to Management. A poster of the racetrack comes alive on the wall behind him. The caption reads "I 'heart' Arcadia", with a heart shape in the center appearing to beat like a live organ.

The scene of the dying girl at the hospital is still fresh in Landon's mind and he wants now more than ever to hold his son in his arms and feel him close and warm and give his thanks to the Universe for the gift of knowing what a bond of unconditional love really feels like. Landon is convinced that the bond between him and his sons (yes, Jason, too, who'll never die to him) holds the entire cosmic firmament in place and without it the galaxies would disintegrate, and the night sky would be full of nothing but shooting stars. He also feels an impulse to express this love in a practical way and the only thing he can think of right now is to buy Tyler an extravagant birthday present. That'll show 'em.

Nick sneaks up on Landon, peeking over his shoulder at his betting card, trying to make it look casual. He's dressed differently today, appears clean and bright, in a dark blue suit and sky-blue dress shirt, as if the scraggly old man became the victim of a complete makeover.

"Hey, Landon, thanks for those betting slips," Nick says.

"What now?"

"Other day, you were here with your boy, had The Lion's Den singled out in the fourth, you gave me the ticket… ring a bell?" Nick says.

"Please don't tell me, I don't wanna know," Landon says, soon as he actually *knows*. "Don't wanna fuckin' know, all right?"

"Say, wanna go in on a pick six?" Nick asks.

"No. I plan on making money today," Landon says.

"What's so special about today?"

"My boy's birthday's coming up. Can't show up empty handed, pretend like I forgot all about it, now can I," Landon says.

Nick marks a horse on his betting card. "Hmm. Elephant In A Room. That's a good name for a horse, a very good name indeed," he says. "Bet on this horse, Landon, I got a good feelin' about it."

The betting booth opens and Landon slips in his betting card and pays, cash on the barrelhead, with the joy of bending under the guillotine.

* * *

Landon spreads out over several seats, up in the nosebleeders close to the Sun. Nick grabs a seat one row above him, blocking Landon's view of the luminary, which is just what the doctor ordered. "How about that earthquake," Landon says, to kill some time.

"One in Northridge, ninety-four?" Nick says.

"Couple hours ago. Must've been all over the news," Landon says.

"No, I watched the news, didn't see nothing. Nobody cares unless it's the Big One," Nick says. "Then we all die anyway."

"I felt it in my bones. A six-point-five at least." Landon looks up but Nick has shifted ever so slightly and a shaft of the sun's light pounds his retina when he least expects it. He shakes his head like someone's just poured scalding water on his face.

"Are you currently on medication?" Nick asks.

"Hey, sorry I brought it up."

"What the hell happened to you anyway?"

"I'd like to know that, too," Landon says.

"You mean you don't remember how you broke your hand, or you mean that in a philosophical kind of way? Like, how did I fuck up my life and ended up here, talking to this old fool," Nick says.

"Yeah, what you said last."

Nick springs up fully erect, like someone has let loose of a coil in his ass, a dark shadow over him. "You call me a fool again, I'll pour this fucking coffee mug right on your face, punk."

Landon assumes a defensive posture. "Sorry, Nick. Jeezuz, what the hell has gotten into you?"

Nick sits right back down, calm as a Buddha all of a sudden. "That's cool, man. Anger with me is like writing on water. That's why you'll never see me with an arm looking like a fuckin' Q-tip."

The horses spring out of the gates for the first race of the day, a blizzard of fury rattling the earth under their hooves. "Hey, wake me up if someone comes looking for me," Landon says, "I think I'm being followed."

"You think you can run, but you can't. Not even in Arcadia," Nick says.

"How's that?"

"You know the old saying, *It'll find you even in Arcadia*," Nick says.

"What?! That's not an old saying," Landon says.

"You ever read that in your fancy books? The old Greeks knew of a paradise, they called it Arcadia," Nick says.

"Oh, yeah, I saw that on a painting," Landon says. "Know all about it."

Nick lets his eyes roam about, as if reminiscing of a golden age he once lived in. "It was inside the Earth, I believe, all green and pastoral, sunny every day, fat sheep grazing about, voluptuous women everywhere, wearing only bikinis, *if that*, no worry in the world, that kinda place. But they said, Death finds you even in Arcadia. There's a Latin phrase to that effect, Et in Arcadia Ego." This jogs Landon's memory to the painting he once saw but he doesn't buy the whole idea wholesale on account of the artist wouldn't go through all that trouble just to state the obvious.

"Bikinis, really?" Landon says.

"I added that part," Nick says, "I do it for effect. I'm a raconteur, man. If you care to know. Either way, you're licked. That's the bottom line."

* * *

By the time the horses blaze through the finish line, Landon is fast asleep. Nick jumps with joy. "Yessss! That's what I'm talking about. Go Elephant! I toldya to bet on this horse, did I not?" He looks down at Landon. "Toldya," he says. "My favorite word in the English language... *toldya*."

Nick pokes Landon, "Landon, who'd you pick in second, huh? Wakey, wakey." Apparently there's no one behind the wheel, so Nick takes the liberty to pluck the ticket out of Landon's pocket. He shakes his head in disappointment. "God, you really have no luck," Nick says.

He then swaps Landon's losing ticket with his own winning one. "Get your kid something nice," Nick says, before heading to the bar.

* * *

It's before the last races of the evening that Landon finally awakes with a start. It takes him a few good seconds to get his bearings, and the first thing he checks for, even before the cash, is his betting slips. He's afraid someone might've taken advantage of an unconscious betting junkie and robbed him of his impending wealth, but his worries are quickly put to rest. Maybe someone really *is* watching over him.

Landon looks up at the monitors showing the race results and, as he paces back and forth in confusion, stares at his betting slips then back to the screens, it finally dawns on him. "What the... Nick... you sonofabitch."

He collects his winnings in cash, and contrary to folk wisdom he does intend to spend it all in one place. Landon figures this will be the grand gesture that'll put him right with Tyler because, let's face it, unconditional reciprocal love notwithstanding, he and Tyler have always been out-of-synch. Landon could use a little bit of doing without doing. Wu wei all the way, baby, just not with Tyler. As the Dao goes.

Not fair to compare Tyler to Jason but things could be a little more simpatico and on the level between two people without the need to put in all that effort. Take, for instance, the day Jason was born. Landon was in the waiting room of the maternity ward at Cedars Sinai, banished there by Melanie, who thought better than have her husband of just six months get exposed to a pussy explosion the kind of which would cure his libido for years to come. And be honest, neither was Landon in the mood to see blood on his firstborn, as he associated blood with other types of horror, like war and disease, and didn't want to forever conflate all these different traumas in his head. So he looked at it as a sacred thing for the mother to go through, and for the child to pass his first initiation into this world, that of arrival upon these shores. All the while he, the father to be, would wait in the wings. Put another way, it wasn't his war to fight. Needless to say, it turned out different.

Landon had just popped open a soda can and slumped back in his chair in the crowded hospital lobby when a sensation of nausea started to creep up in his body. He first thought it was something he ate, or maybe just the nerves but, before he could get into it more analytically, he'd already dropped the Diet Coke on the carpet floor and shot straight up like a puppet in the hands of an invisible puppeteer. With determined strides he covered the distance to Melanie's ward in no time, winding down the labyrinthine hallways like he was a resident robot, guided by remote control. "The baby's suffocating," he announced, as he burst into the room, with a voice that he felt came out of a different body. That drew a chuckle from the Nurse, who explained to him that it was normal for the monitors to lose the baby's heartbeat as he was slinking down the tunnel. But Landon would have none of that and started screaming through the open door, "We need a fuckin' doctor in here, *now*! The baby's suffocating," causing Melanie to cry and beg for him to leave before making a scene. Sure enough, an army of doctors soon invaded the delivery room only to ascertain that, indeed, the mother's bladder was full, and it was pressing against the baby's head, suffocating him. A middle-aged doctor quickly inserted a catheter to drain the bladder, something that should've been done before the epidural but was somehow overlooked, and had they allowed even one more minute to go by it would've been too late. When the cyanotic bluish baby came out and the whole drama subsided, a moment of quiet enveloped the room and they all turned to Landon and asked, "How did you know?" Landon simply shrugged, as he had no explanation or prior experience of such things, but he knew it then and there that he and his baby boy were bound by a chain of breath and stardust reaching beyond time, beyond reason, beyond life and death. He picked up the baby and held him in his arms, a miracle covered in ichor.

* * *

Big Ben runs a brush over the side of his racehorse like an automaton who's only mastered one skill. "Sorry about the other day. Guy can be a prick sometimes," Big Ben says. Landon surveys the hangar, the lash of Rocanna's harsh words still floating in the air around him. "Don't mention it," Landon says.

"How did you make out today?" Big Ben asks.

"Did okay, thanks to crazy Nick. Don't know what got into that guy… Never heard him string two sentences together, all of a sudden he sounds like Lao fuckin' Tzu," Landon says. "Hey, I'm looking to buy my kid a horse, like for his birthday."

Big Ben laughs. "What do you mean, buy him a horse? It's not that simple."

"I don't mean like a regular size horse. I mean like a miniature one, for kids."

"How about a pony?"

"A pony, that'll do. I heard they brought a bunch of horses over from Hollywood Park, now that they closed shop over there," Landon says, and starts peeking over to the other stalls, the fat roll of cash in his pocket giving him a sense of entitlement, like strolling around a used car lot thinking, I can have any o' these clunkers.

"You'd still need to board the pony, y'know, find a place to keep it, feed it, curry it, take it out for a walk, don't know what to tell you, high maintenance," Big Ben says. "You can't just buy a pony like you buy a fuckin' dog, throw it a bone in the back yard and let it howl at the moon."

"Well, let me worry about that," Landon says.

"Why don't you just bring your kid over in the offseason? I'll teach him how to feed a horse, how to ride it," Big Ben says.

"Anybody can take a kid out for a damn pony ride. Take him out to Griffith Park or some place, have him ride the carousel…" Landon says, less in reply to Big Ben than a continuation of the argument he's been carrying around in his head with Ray. "That's easy, but give the boy something he'd remember for the rest of his life, how's that? Everybody remembers their first pet, like a first love or something. Now, that's special. And this cute little pony here, this would be Tyler's first pet, animal familiar, or emotional support animal or whateverthefuck."

Landon knows that from his first son, Jason. Soon as he started talking and up to the age of five that boy pestered Landon nonstop about getting a pet. A puppy, to be more precise, the boy wanted a puppy real bad. Landon resisted the assault, coming up with sundry excuses, citing living conditions, apartment life and such, the high maintenance of the animal, which is only a puppy for a short time before it grows into a beast, but eventually had to give in to the relentless pressure. Driven to exasperation he walked into a pet store one day and bought a *goldfish*. He took it home in its little fish tank and a week's supply of fish food, which looked like ant turds. He brought Jason home from pre-K that day and had him walk to the fish tank with his eyes closed for the big reveal. Jason was giddy with excitement, pricking up his ears in anticipation of the baby barks, until he opened his eyes, and it was like someone dimmed the lights in the room. "What's the matter, you don't like it?" Landon asked. "Yes, I like it, it's really cute. What's its name?" Jason asked, pointing to the goldfish. "Its name is *Puppy*!" Landon said, smiling proudly. Jason quickly took a shine to that goldfish, so much in fact that for fear of having it miss a meal he accidentally overfed it and found it belly up one day and started wailing at the shock of losing something close to his heart for the first time in his life and Landon felt compelled to explain to his son, in words he'd understand, the nature of Life and Death and the cycles of the eternal return and together they arranged a burial at sea ceremony for Puppy, although instead of driving to the ocean at peak traffic hour Landon suggested they flush Puppy down the toilet, whereupon Landon also felt compelled to explain to Jason the workings of the pipes and the waterways and canals and sewers and how all that water travels in labyrinthine ways to both nourish and cleanse but eventually it all flows into the oceans and the seas.

* * *

"So can you help a brother out?" Landon asks Big Ben. The jockey nods, the wheels already in motion. "It'll cost you." Landon flashes his fresh roll of cash and, he could swear, Big Ben looks a good five inches taller for a second.

"You certainly got my attention," Big Ben says.

Big Ben opens the doors to a hangar nearby. Ponies left and right, one more adorable than the next, at least to Landon's eyes. He senses their loneliness and vows to use the power of the purse to rescue one of them from that pain. He looks around for the winner of that golden ticket.

"This here's a pinto patterned Chincoteague pony," Big Ben says.

"Man, they're cute as hell. My boy would love one of these," Landon says.

"Friendly too, considering."

Landon draws near to the pony and pets it. "Considering what?"

"They're born in the wild, on an island," Big Ben says, reeling Landon in like a used car salesman.

"How do they end up here?" Landon asks.

"Pony penning."

"Okay—"

"Local firemen herd 'em across the shallow waters at slack tide. Take 'em from one island to another, then auction off the foals. Rain or shine, they go swimming across that channel, into the unknown," Big Ben recites like a Shakespearean actor, letting those last words reverberate in the quiet of the hangar.

"Oh, man, I bet you that scares the hell outta them. No wonder they look so, I don't know, despondent," Landon says.

"They ain't exactly going to the slaughterhouse, y'know," Big Ben says.

"Yeah, but *they* don't know that. It's the fear of the unknown," Landon says. "Reason why people are afraid of Death."

"God knows what goes on in their cute little pony heads, but it's a sight to see. Your boy might like to see that spectacle one day," Big Ben says.

"All right, I'll take this one. Sold!" Landon counts some bills and hands them over to Big Ben.

"That's just for the pony, you understand. You need a stable to keep it in," Big Ben says, catching Landon staring at the hundred-dollar bill that survived the transaction. "I'm talking rent here, down payment, first and last month," Big Ben continues, "and that," meaning the bill, "won't do."

"Hey, look, I ain't done for the day. Let me come back later. For the rent on the pony house, I mean. The money's out there at the track, there's a bunch of suckers holding onto *my* money, thinking it's their money but they're wrong, and all I gotta do is go claim it," Landon says.

"The pony can stay here for a couple days, okay? No longer," Big Ben says. "After that, your rent is due, or you got yourself a fuckin' house pet."

"I'm on a hot streak, man, can't you see? My luck has been turning. And besides, maybe I wanna give my feral pony more suitable digs than what I'm seeing here," Landon says, "No offense."

"Like what?"

"I don't know," Landon says. "He just don't look too happy here. Look at his eyes. He's about to cry. I wanna bring him closer to home, close to my boy."

"Tsk-tsk." Big Ben shakes his head, as if suspecting this whole thing is gonna end in tears.

"Maybe I should take him out for a ride later. You know, like a test ride? What do you think about that?" Landon asks.

"Where to?"

Landon shrugs. "There's a 7-11 down the street. I can get him some sugar."

Big Ben laughs. "Yeah, I'd like to see that."

"Well, could I?"

"Ain't no law against it," Big Ben says, "Come to think of it, in traffic you have the right of way."

"How about that," Landon says, as he spreads his good hand into a rake and gently curries the pony. "You hear that, lil pony? We have the right of way."

"Suit yourself, Landon. He's *your* fucking problem now," Big Ben says.

* * *

Landon wades, as if in slow motion, through the clouds of cigarette smoke, past the degenerate gamblers and lowlifes, past the lucky few, past the unlucky many, past the worker bees, past the blood suckers, until he reaches the betting booth, collects a small rainy day stash out of a secret pocket, and marks his pick for the last race of the day, going all in, as it were, for the right to the Chincoteague pony's world headquarters.

Landon follows that race with renewed interest. "Goddamn, you run like a fuckin' pony!!" he yells a few times out of sheer desperation but, alas, the poor animals can't understand a word he's saying. He cuts a forlorn figure on his way out of Arcadia, and like a fallen angel he glances back with vengeance and a promise to return some day, although deep down a feeling grows, running counter to that thought, that he won't. It gnaws at him the same way it did when he said his good-byes to Jason the day of that fateful trip, somehow knowing it would be the last time he'd see his boy alive, like there's something inside him that can see through his past and future equally well, but its voice is muted by desire and resentment.

*"His body is yellow in color,
    he holds a wish-fulfilling jewel in his hand
and sits on a horse-throne."*

The Tibetan Book of the Dead, Day Three

The back hatch of the horse trailer rattles open. A horse handler steps inside to inspect the package before delivery then lowers down a ramp for the animal to exit its temporary cage on wheels.

"Welcome home, hoss," Landon says to the Chincoteague pony. "Don't worry, you'll get a proper name soon."

The handler carefully takes the pony out and hands the reins to Landon. "You sure about this?" Landon slips him some cash for the trouble. He waits until the truck takes off then snatches the harness and looks the pony in the eyes, as if to convey that what is about to happen is nothing more than establishing a contract between them, two sentient beings at once at odds with the Universe and yet flowing downstream with the rest of the flotsam.

He then walks the animal to the nearest available parking meter.

The spot is somewhat shaded and street traffic is sparse enough to Landon's satisfaction, as he doesn't need to worry about the pony suffering in the heat on top of the humiliation and everything else. He doesn't plan on leaving the animal there for too long, but just the right amount of time for him to play up the surprise in Tyler's impressionable mind. So, he ties the pony to the pole and makes sure to feed the meter to the hilt, two hours on the nose.

"Be right back, buddy," he says, "and don't be afraid of the passing cars, they're just like horses but made out of metal, they're here to keep you company. They got horses on the *inside*, where you can't see them, but trust me, they're there." He pats the pony on the back and rushes up the flight of stairs to Melanie's apartment, giddy with excitement.

Landon hardly gets a chance to close the door behind him when Melanie drags him near to her, as if to shank him. "You won't believe what happened," she says.

"What."

"The cigarette truck I told you about the other day," she gets a blank look off of Landon, then continues, "the one I went to the docks on my day off to personally oversee, so that nothing would go wrong with the transport…"

Landon plays dumb. "Oh, yeah, I remember. What about it?"

"Someone jacked it," Melanie says.

"Whoa." Landon actually takes a step back, as if to better absorb the shocking news.

"Can you believe it?" Melanie says.

"Hey, don't say I didn't warn you," Landon says. "And, if you asking me about it… but I don't wanna beat on a dead horse."

"I know, I know. Ray's been acting real strange lately."

"So you think he might have had something to do with it?"

"I don't know, Landon. Be honest with you, I'm really confused. I try to talk to him, and he just turns away, doesn't even look at me. Like it's my fault or something."

"Well, look, the guy's an asshole, obviously. You did nothing to deserve this kind of treatment," Landon says, "Besides, he'll get his money back from insurance anyway."

"Not really. That's why he's pissed," Melanie says.

"What do you mean? You let the policy lapse, or what?" Landon asks, now genuinely curious about this turn of events.

"No, Landon, it's not that… Insurance only covers what's on the manifest, you understand? The manifest and the cargo packaging were rigged for Ray to pay lower import taxes," Melanie says.

"Okay, so what's on the manifest?"

"Toilet paper. Made in China. Worth as much shit as you can wipe with it," Melanie says.

"Ouch! Sorry to hear that, really," Landon says, and places his good hand on her shoulder to comfort her, "if you need someone to talk to I could come by later tonight. After you put Tyler to sleep, I'm thinking might be a good time."

"I'm fine, really. Just had to get it off my chest, that's all," she says.

"Remember, I'm here for you, I want you to know that no matter what," Landon says, and steals a hug from her.

Landon generally has no qualms about lying to her so long as it serves a greater good, and survival of his family is nothing but axiomatic in his view. He's only just becoming more aware of the lengths he would go to, to accomplish that. Stealing a truckload of cigarettes seems like a trifle in retrospect, he'd do it again in a flash. As long as no one gets hurt, it's just stuff, molecules moving from one place to another, money changing hands, the world stays the same and no one really gives a shit. Lying to his ex-wife about it is just harmless fibbing, on par with her claiming she's on the rag two weeks in a row.

There's a long list of things whose real meaning Landon has misunderstood, but at the top of that list is something called the Doctrine of Skillful Means, a Buddhist concept that his newly minted girlfriend Stephanie tried to explain to him one day, might've even been on their first date, but didn't go very far on account of she didn't grasp it either. To Landon's surprise, one thing led to another and before he knew it they were both naked on her kitchen floor, Landon employing all manner of skillful means to get her to climax, but she was a tough customer to the bitter end.

Afterwards she elaborated on the subject, while puffing on a post-coital joint. "Back in the Buddha's day, a long time ago, like before fire trucks and water hoses, the house of this nobleman dude lit up like a Christmas tree. This is before Christmas trees, but anyway... He'd dropped a cigarette on the carpet, and all of a sudden there were flames everywhere and his kids, 'cause he had like three or four kids, they're all playing around with god knows what, model trains and... no wait, that can't be... okay, they're playing with wooden sticks or something, but the dude's like 'Hey kids, let's get the fuck outta here, but pronto!' But the kids, they were like 'no, Dad, we're having so much fun playing with these wooden sticks, we don't wanna go anywhere.' And the dude says to them 'hey kids, look around you, there's fire everywhere', but the kids didn't know what fire meant cause they'd never seen fire before. They lived a cloistered, carefree life. Then he says, 'hey kids, you stupid little fucks, if we don't leave right this second we're all gonna fucking die', but the kids didn't know what Death was, cause all they did all day was play stupid games, and besides they were too young to know anyway. Finally, the dude says, 'hey kids, waiting right outside that door are the latest model wooden chariots and all kinds of fly toys that are so cool you can't even imagine'. And soon as they heard that, the kids rushed outside and were saved from the fire. Well, they were pretty pissed when they didn't find any toys waiting for them outside, but their father made up for it later and took 'em to Toys "R" Us, well y'know the Flintstones version, and got 'em like a cartful of toys. Now here's the question... Do you find the dad's actions deceitful? Cause I don't. I guess the moral of the story is it's okay to use skillful means sometimes, like when someone's life depends on it... Anyway, the Buddha himself told that story or parable, whatever, to anyone who cared to listen... though *maybe* not exactly in those words," she said before putting out the blunt of her joint and nudging closer to Landon. "Hey, I'm still kinda horny, wanna fuck again?"

Lesson learned. Landon can't help now but feel really proud of his application of skillful means to save Melanie and their child from a future with a man of despicable character and hair on his back sticking out from under his shirt collar for chrissakes, a future worse than death. The motherfucker's shedding hair on Landon's couch worse than a gray wolf. The couch Landon paid for in blood and tears. Jeezuz. And if that entailed his stealing a cargo of cigarettes, plus the truck itself, then so be it. It ain't like he was gonna take the money and run to some tropical island with a fake passport and a fake blonde on his arm, that's not his endgame. This was done out of sheer necessity, he had to resort to this sort of thing because he had no other options. After all he's done for his country, there's no recourse for a man of his talents and capabilities, a truly great man. Come to think of it, he's the *victim* here. So his reasoning goes. P.S. Fuck Ray Barba and the horse he rode in on. Sincerely, Landon Briggs.

"What the hell happened to your hand?" Melanie asks, like really seeing him for the first time. She holds Landon's hand and tries to peek under the bandage to ascertain the damage. The painkillers have started to wear off and he groans with pain. "Oh, it's nothing."

"You got into a fight again, didn't you?"

"There wasn't much of a fight," Landon says, looking away as if to avert the light of the Sun on a hot summer day. "Actually, you won't believe this, but I was thinking about you... last night, y'know, and I guess I got a little over-excited, if you know what I mean," he says with a laugh, motioning his hand up and down in a stroking motion.

"I should see the other guy, right?" Melanie says.

"Oh, no, the other guy's fine, trust me. He's ready for another round."

Melanie smiles as she grabs Landon's crotch so hard a tear rolls down his cheek. "That's what you get for lying to me," she says.

Landon misses that easy-going banter between them, the back-and-forth that keeps him on his toes, the subtle ways she'd let him know she's not buying into any of his bullshit while at the same time giving him enough rope to hang himself with while she watches bemusedly, like a freak show spectator, without lifting a single finger.

"You know what I'm talking about, don't you?" she says.

Landon senses that Melanie's trying to steer the conversation into perilous territory by way of an implied accusation, and he immediately deflects it best he can. "Goddammit, Mel, that hurts," he says, letting her think that he possibly didn't even register her loaded remark, and then promptly turns to Tyler's room, knowing that being within Tyler's ear strike is a safe zone for heated arguments, at least as far as Melanie's concerned. "What's the little one doing?" he asks.

"He was playing some video game earlier."

"I thought you had strict house rules against that sort of thing," he shouts before quickly checking himself back to a whisper. "A boy his age ought to spend more time in the real world."

"He felt tired, so I let him play for a while," Melanie says.

"Is he all right?"

"He's a little jaundiced, but he's getting better."

"Why didn't you tell me he was sick?" Landon asks. She looks up at him until their eyes lock for good and says, "I don't tell you a lot of things."

No kidding. As if Landon needs any more confirmation that this woman would forever be a mystery to him.

"So, did you get him a present?" she presses on, "He's gonna be very disappointed, you didn't bring him something."

"What kind of father do you think I am?"

* * *

A crudely pixelated horse runs an obstacle course to the accompaniment of various calliope sound effects for each time the horse crashes on the track, which is often. Yet again, the horse and its rider land face down in the dirt. This looping simulation game strikes Landon as uncannily life-like in its repetitive tedium.

"C'mon, Dad, is that the best you can do?" Tyler says, exasperated by his dad's lack of focus.

Tyler wipes his runny nose with his yellow T-shirt and reaches for the controls, but Landon would have none of that. He's gonna give it one more shot, even with his bum hand cramping his style. "One last time. I can do this," Landon says. The horse approaches another hurdle but just like before it crashes straight into it.

"Oh, man. You keep making the same mistake, dad," Tyler says, shaking his head, "You release too early. How'd you expect to get better if—"

"This is stupid," Landon says, the frustration getting to him. "Can't you, like, go *around* the obstacles?"

"First thing I learned about these games, Dad, is if you run into obstacles it means you're on the right track. That's how you score points, you know."

Landon tosses the controller at Tyler. "*You* play. I'm done with this crap. Leave me out of it." But Tyler looks at his dad with a maturity that belies his years. "You'll never get to the next level if you keep making the same mistakes," the boy says. Landon notices a subtle change in Tyler's delivery, it's as if he's momentarily possessed by a much older entity, as if a wise wind blew over the little boy and accessed a state of his being present only in an eternity beyond this life. He immediately regrets his petulance, which made *him* look the child by comparison. He quickly tries to restore order into the world by planting a fatherly kiss on Tyler's cheek and thus forgive the boy's childish ways. "Who cares about this," Landon says, "it's a dumb simulation game."

"What does that mean—*simulation*?"

"Means it's not real. It's not real life, it doesn't hurt. It's just an imitation of the real thing," Landon says.

"But you can still learn from it."

"If you say so." Landon moves to the window and parts the blinds. He curses under his breath, "Dumb fuckin' game," and as he peers out the window he could swear the pony's staring straight back at him. It's Tyler's voice that snaps him out of it, "Dad?" He turns to Tyler, "What?"

"Where's *your* dad?"

"Well, funny you should ask," Landon says, and takes a seat back on the bed next to Tyler. "He passed away last week."

"It's not funny."

"It's just a figure of speech, didn't mean nothing by it."

"How come I've never met your father?" Tyler asks.

"He just wasn't always a good person to be around. He didn't like people too much."

"Are *you* a good person?"

At this point Landon's definitely thinking there must be something wrong with the boy, no doubt going back to the humiliating scene at the racetrack, but just the same he indulges him in the conversation for the sole purpose of surprising *himself*. Which he does when he says, "Well, I spent the last few days thinking about just that, and guess what?" The boy shrugs. "I'm coming back home," Landon says.

"When, *today*?"

"Not today, in a week or two," Landon says with paternal authority, "I gotta take care of some things first, but it's pretty much settled."

"That's great news, Dad," Tyler says. "I wonder why Mom didn't mention anything." It's that tone *again*, the hint of a deeper understanding of the game being played that puts Landon on the back foot. "Well, she's probably waiting to surprise you, so keep this between you and me." Landon couldn't change the subject fast enough. "So I hear you went to Griffith Park the other day."

"Yes," Tyler says.

Landon parts the blinds and looks out at the leashed pony, the sun beating mercilessly down on it. The pony twitches its rear nervously and appears to dance as a delivery truck rushes by, and it reminds Landon of the scared wild burros jumping at the sound of fireworks on the Tijuana streets on a balmy day some years ago, but that's another story. It also reminds him of the Surfliner he took to San Diego some time before that, on his way to visit a wounded buddy at the Naval Medical Center. The train shook and screeched when it hit the brakes on a curving track and the whistles blew clear to the Moon, and Landon jolted out of his nap, seated as he was in the caboose and in perfect view of the locomotive, whereabouts he spotted a herd of about five or six wild horses, probably Mexican, nonchalantly crossing the tracks in complete oblivion of the danger heading their way. One horse after another stepped over the lines, the train inching ever closer, the herd almost completely in the safe but for the last member, a young buck feeling its oats in the world, almost daring the metal monster to a deathly game of tag. The train hit the daredevil squarely in the hind legs, flinging its rear off the tracks and causing it to spin around full circle. The horse stayed upright, though badly shaken, and as Landon's car was slowly approaching, he first thought the horse might have dodged a bullet but that was not the case. It tried to step on its hind legs but all they did was this funny step-dance, as if near something too hot to the touch, and when the horse spun around again, Landon spotted the vertical gash on its side, blood and entrails already bubbling out of the two-foot opening. They shoot horses for a lot less than that and it stood to reason that, especially out there in the wild with the coyotes lurking, the animal's fate was sealed. The rest of the herd seemed to sense that as they gathered around the wounded one, their heads gently touching each other's in a sensual dance of nudging and caressing, feeling the last warm drop of a life before growing cold, learning about Death in their own way. It's the last image Landon saw before the train whooshed away to its own destination. Landon believed in omens and understood that he was given the privilege to witness that incident as a way to prepare him for what was coming. He just didn't know yet how all the pieces would fit together in the end.

* * *

Landon thinks to put the Chincoteague pony out of its temporary misery and spring the surprise on his boy and get it over with but there's still something gnawing at him, something he can't quite let go of. "Mom take you there?"

"Mom and Ray," the boy says with a sigh, as if knowing what to expect next. "Oh, really. Mom and Ray…" Landon says. "And did you have fun at the park? With Mom and Ray?"

"It was all right. Ray took me to the pony rides. It was pretty cool," the boy says, then quickly qualifies his statement, probably realizing that a birthday present might be on the line, "I mean, I like horses and the horses were cool."

"Did you tell him that was the most fun you've ever had," Landon asks, his voice trembling with buried anger. The boy is squirming under the pressure, and Landon drills him again. "Well, did you tell him that?"

"I don't remember, Dad."

"Think harder."

"I told him I had fun."

"Most fun ever? *Ever*-ever?" Landon asks, and when Tyler drops his head Landon knows the answer. "Really, you sound like a sissy now, too," Landon says. "What's the matter with you?"

"I'm sorry," Tyler says, fighting back tears. Landon realizes he's once again gone too far, and he sits beside him and puts his arm around him, which naturally only helps Tyler open up the floodgates. It's a good five minutes before the boy returns to neutral, another five minutes for the poor pony to suffer out there in the asphalt jungle.

Landon points to a wooden horse in the corner of the room. "That's new. Where did you get that?"

"The flea market," the boy says, his mood instantly changing for the better.

"Nice. What kinda horse is it?"

"Wooden. It's a wooden horse." This draws a laugh from Landon and then Tyler follows suit, just happy to laugh along with his dad than at anything particularly funny.

"What's his name?"

"I named him Ulysses," the boy says, proudly.

"Of course," Landon says, "Do you know what a Chincoteague pony is?"

"Nope."

Images of ponies crossing a shallow channel flash across the computer screen. "They call it pony penning," Landon explains to the boy, "You see all those people up there in the rafters," he continues, "That's gonna be us next July. What do you think about that?"

"You promise?" Tyler asks.

"Course I promise. And I'll do you one better. I got a surprise for you."

Tyler gives him a quick frisk but comes up empty. "What is it? Tell me already."

Landon stands up and, just as he's about to make the big reveal, he hears the front door open and then close, followed by a man's voice. An unfortunately familiar voice.

"I can't believe this," Landon says, "What's that moron doing here?"

"That's Ray, Dad."

"Yeah, I know my morons like you know your A-B-C's. You wanna go say hi to your new best friend?"

Landon asks, but the boy knows better than to be drawn in. "No?" Landon says, "Never? *Ever* ever?"

Melanie sticks her head into the room to address Landon. "Ray and I are gonna step out in a minute. Can you watch Tyler for a couple hours?"

"Sure," Landon says, then down to a whisper, "Does Ray know I'm here?"

"Yeah, I just told him," she says. "Is there a problem?" Then Landon hears Ray yell out from the kitchen in a voice loud enough to cause a minor temblor. "Hey, Melanie, some clown tied up a pony to the parking meter, you believe that?"

"Did *what*?" Melanie asks.

"Tell Tyler to come over here. He's gonna get a kick outta this," Ray says, to Landon's increasing frustration.

Landon tells Tyler to stay put in his room and keep his door closed, while he goes over to take care of some pressing business. He finds Ray and Melanie standing by the kitchen window, looking in the direction of the pony. "Can you guys keep it *down* here?"

"What's the problem," Ray wants to know.

"That's *my* fucking pony out there, okay?" Landon says, trying hard to contain himself, "It's a surprise birthday present for Tyler, and you just ruined it, man."

"What were you thinking, Landon?" Melanie chimes in, "And where the hell are you gonna keep the pony, anyway?"

"Maybe Tyler and the pony can share a bunk bed. I don't know," Landon says.

"Tsk-tsk, that's just the most irresponsible thing," Ray says, slowly winding Landon up. "You're clearly not thinking ahead."

"Just mind your own business, Ray," Landon says.

"Landon, answer me," Melanie insists, "What do you plan to do with that poor horse?"

"He turns everything he touches into shit," Ray says, and Landon's about to unload on him when he hears Tyler's voice.

"I saw a pony outside, tied up to a parking meter," Tyler says from the safety of the hallway.

"Take him back to his room for a minute, please," Landon says to Melanie and she's on it.

Alone now, Ray leans into Landon, "Where's my fucking truck?"

"Safe place. Don't worry about it."

Ray reaches into his pockets, flings a cell phone and a wallet at Landon. "Your wallet and such." Landon quickly inspects it. "Where's the cash? I had like fifty-five dollars in here."

"Safe place. Don't worry about it."

"Oh, you made a little joke," Landon says, pocketing the wallet. "Your goon still at my place?"

"No. I can always find you if I need to. No town's big enough for a fool like you," Ray says, as he moves to within an inch of Landon's face, grabs him by the throat and pins him against the wall. "Bring the truck back to Lex's place *tonight*... Never mind tonight, it'd look suspicious if you left Tyler's birthday party, so let's say by tomorrow night, and I'll forget this ever happened."

Landon reaches beside him with his good hand, opens a drawer and grabs a steak knife which he prods Ray with just enough to know it's there. "Melanie has no idea what a fucking crook you are, or she'd never marry you. I know you killed people. Or had the Diadora brothers do it for you, makes no difference. I heard all about it," Landon says. Ray eases back as the business end of the knife pricks his side. "Is that a threat?" Ray asks.

"A proposal, more like," Landon says. "You cancel the wedding, get out of her life, *our lives*, you can have your truck back. Cigarettes, too."

"No deal," Ray says.

"Just think it over. You got until, I dunno, tomorrow night."

Melanie steps back inside. "Everything all right?" Landon casually puts the steak knife back in the drawer. Ray peeks out the window, like nothing has transpired. "Hey, Landon, I think your pony's about to get a parking ticket."

Landon runs out of the building like it's on fire, checks his step as he skids by the double-parked cruiser and approaches the police officer.

"I'm Officer McGowen, LAPD," the cop says, "This your horse, sir?"

"Yeah, that's my *vehicle*," Landon says. "Is there a problem?"

The cop circles around the pony. "We got calls that your vehicle here has been acting nervously, so we had to check it out," the cop says. "It looks like the animal's not used to sitting in traffic. You're gonna have to move it outta here before it gets hurt or it hurts someone."

Melanie and Tyler come out to join the block party. The boy makes a beeline to the pony. "You got him for me, daddy?"

"Ain't it a beauty," Landon says, beaming with pride. "Happy birthday, son!"

Tyler tries to wrap his arms around the little horse. "Yes, he's beautiful. He's a Chincoteague pony, isn't he?"

"That's right. And what do you think it'd be a good name for him?" The boy grabs the pony's head in his tiny hands and tries to make it look at him. "How are you, Agamemnon? I'm Tyler."

"I don't know what the hell you were thinking, Landon," Melanie says, "Where're we gonna keep this thing?"

"I don't know, yet, you're putting all this pressure on me now," he says. "I guess I wanted to see if he likes it first. Worry about all that other stuff later."

"Of course I love it," Tyler says, caressing the animal.

The scene attracts some curious stragglers and there's presently a small crowd of rubberneckers waiting for the grand finale. "Sir, you'll have to move the horse now," the cop says. "Do you understand?"

"Are they gonna take Agamemnon away, Dad?" the boy asks in full panic mode.

"No, Tyler. No one's taking the pony away from you," Landon says.

"Do you plan to ride it out of here, sir?" the cop wants to know.

"No law against it," Landon says. "Come to think of it, the horse has the right of way, doesn't he?"

"Yes, he does," the cop says.

"You hear that, Tyler? You get on top of this pony and you're King of the Road," Landon says, proudly patting the rear of the horse. "Can't wait to take him out for a ride, Dad," Tyler says, circling around the pony with excitement.

"Well, if the pony gets spooked and you get hit by a car, that doesn't make you any less dead," the cop says, "So I suggest you get on it right now if you want to beat the traffic."

"Look, Officer, it's my kid's birthday," Landon says. "You know how it is. Just got him a nice present, this pony here. Cost me a pretty penny, not that you care. He'd be very disappointed if he didn't get to play with it just for a little while... You don't wanna be the one to crush a boy's dream, do you. Now, what do you say you close an eye, I'll be outta here before sundown."

"Listen, sir," the cop says, evidently annoyed by this intrusion into his busy schedule of fighting actual crime, "I have no time or disposition to argue with you. If you're not on the horse by the time I reach for my handcuffs, I'm taking you in."

"Whoa, whoa, now," Landon protests, "All you need to do is close your eyes for a few minutes, go back into your cruiser and take a nap or something, I'm not hurting anyone here." Landon puts his hands on the cop's forearm, preventing him from unfastening the pair of handcuffs tied to his belt and, to make matters worse, the pony drops a big dump, as if on cue, which splatters all over the cop's pants. They turn in unison, look down at the pile of manure on the ground and know right away how this is gonna end.

"Oh, Jeezuz," the cop says, "That's it! You're going with me." He has the cuffs ready and turns Landon around, his arms on the pony. "No need for that. I'll clean up, officer," Landon says, his face flush against the saddle.

"Listen, I don't care what you're trying to do here, but you're breaking all kinds of laws," the cop says.

"Well, you ask me, I think the law should obey *us*," Landon says, not helping his cause one bit, his hands wrung into the tight cuffs.

"What about the pony, daddy?" Tyler cries out.

"Animal services will take care of the horse unless you have a place for it," the cop says, as he shoves Landon into the back of the cruiser.

Tyler starts to cry, his dream present being taken away as unexpectedly as it had arrived. The cop makes a call to dispatch, and Landon yells something about bail money from the back of the car, but Melanie appears to not quite hear, or care to hear, what he has said.

Melanie drags a distraught Tyler back into the building without so much as a goodbye. When the cruiser takes off, Landon scans the windows of the apartment for any sign of Tyler peeking out to wave goodbye, but the boy is nowhere to be seen, and in that moment Landon feels more alone than ever, still trying to figure out how everything has turned out so wrong, so quickly. He had nothing but the best intentions after all.

Landon ends up at the North Hollywood station where he's charged with animal endangerment and resisting arrest. He knows it would be futile to plead with Melanie for bail money after making such a scene, so he uses his phone call to alert Stephanie instead. She's habitually late and this day is no different, so Landon ends up spending the night in a holding cell together with two other men.

One is a wiry youth wearing a baggy, plain, used-to-be-white T-shirt, fresh out of puberty judging by the fuzz on his chin standing for what's supposed to be a beard, and a rotten attitude to go with it. Says his name is Lewis, and when Landon asks him if it's Lewis like 'Lewis and Clarke' or Louis as in 'Louis Armstrong', he says he don't know any of those fellas, but he'd ask around. The other inmate is a frail, pale man in his sixties, dressed in a suit about two sizes too large and reeking of cheap booze. He introduces himself as Duncan Pettibon and lets Landon know more than once that he used to work as an investment advisor at a bank out in Westwood, a bank not to be named to protect the *guilty*, ha-ha. Says he took out an early retirement and decided to spend more time with his family, which he had neglected in his years dedicated to speculative profits. Sadly, he'd come to regret his decision, as it turned out his family wasn't all that keen on spending more time with him in the first place, so he came to see his days as a banker as the good ol' days.

"Every morning for two whole weeks," Duncan reminisces, "I'd walk to work right past these big windows at the Hammer Museum—"

"They got a museum for hammers? Where at, man? I gotta see that for myself," Lewis (or Louis) says as he barges in.

"It's an art museum, Hammer's just the name of the rich crook it was named after. Like how they name a street, so they name museums," Duncan says, slightly annoyed by the intrusion. "So I'd walk by and stop for a few minutes to watch four Tibetan monks put together a huge sand mandala. In the morning they're working on it, at lunchtime they're plugging away, and when I'd leave work they're still going at it, hovering over the thing, dropping tiny grains of colored sand onto the big table."

"I love me some sand castles," Lewis says, "I take my lil girl, she about two and half now, take her to the beach ev'ry other Sunday, spend the whole day building sand castles, don't need no Tibetan monk show me how it's done."

"Can I finish my goddamn story, kid," Duncan says, trying to browbeat the boy.

"Oh, go right ahead, ol' man. Thought you was done with the story."

"Sunrise to sundown," Duncan continues, "the monks are there doing this tedious work and I'd watch them drop tiny colored grains until a pattern emerged. Day after day, the same meticulous work until, at the end of the two weeks, the work is completed. I remember the thrill of it when I was finally able to see the finished work, all the little patterns flowing into the large one like rivers into the sea. It was the most beautiful thing I'd ever seen. Still is. It filled me with a strange feeling, can't put it into words. I couldn't stop thinking about it over the weekend, so on the morning of the following Monday I stopped by the museum to see it again."

"The Museum of Hammers?" Lewis/Louis says in a low enough voice to make it easy for Duncan to ignore him.

"I was sure the mandala would become the main attraction, perfect as it was," Duncan says, "but no, it turns out that the mandala I'd seen on Friday wasn't the finished work at all. In fact, as I'd soon realize, it was far from perfect." He pauses there and lets that thought hang like bait.

"What happened to it?" Lewis/Louis asks, genuinely intrigued.

"Once the sand mandala was finished, the monks took it out to the Santa Monica pier or thereabouts and ceremoniously dumped it into the ocean," the banker says with a laugh.

"What I tell ya, man," Lewis/Louis says, jumping off the bench, "Sand castles! Shit, I knew where this was going, sorry to ruin the ending for y'all. So what they call sand castles in Tibetanese, again?" he asks.

"Mandalas... but they're not sand castles, they're something else. They're patterns flowing out from a center. I don't know what to tell you, kid, just look it up on your electronic gadgets and you'll see," Duncan says.

"After all that work, huh," Landon says, his first words of the night.

"Imagine that," the banker says. "The most beautiful thing I've ever seen."

The inmates enjoy a few moments of silence, each contemplating the story in his way, twisting and turning it into something that makes sense to them.

"Mind if I ask," Landon says after some time, "what'd they bring you in here for?"

"Exposing myself... Westfield Fashion Square, second floor bridge... *Allegedly*," Duncan says, matter-of-factly.

"Oh, wow," Landon manages.

"Tell you something, gentlemen," Duncan says, and stands up like he's ready to give a commencement speech, "these days we live in, people just don't know what the fuck beauty is any more." He then shouts "Hammer time!", and quickly drops his pants to reveal his nakedness and stamp his inmates with permanent burns on their retinas, leaving Landon to wonder if Beauty is indeed in the eye of the beholder or we just simply see what we are.

"The soft yellow light
　　of
the hungry ghosts
will also shine."

The Tibetan Book of the Dead, Day Four

Twenty odd years on, the house has lost whatever shine it once had and an "Unsafe" red-tag notice is stuck to the front door, a deterrent to potential buyers more than anything. Situated on top of a knoll in a quaint equestrian zoned area snuggled between Burbank and Glendale, the house still claims a rustic charm and summons up the remembrance of a time gone by.

Bernie Stein Esq, property lawyer with offices near all major freeways, unlocks the front door for Landon. Bernie sniffles constantly while he speaks, and his words are accompanied by a wheezing sound, as if his lungs have been punctured. "I couldn't bring myself to see your father like that. Please don't take it the wrong way," Bernie says, adjusting his yellow tie, which glares like the sun against the black backdrop of his suit.

"It's not... how you say it, *kosher*, right?" Landon says. "I get it, man, don't worry about it."

Landon has only a vague recollection of Bernie going back to the time Mr. Briggs bought his first pedigreed horse. He'd had a few horses before Bardo Hollywood, but Mr. Briggs used them mainly for leisure and some film work, something he had to do to complement his Vietnam vet pension, which by itself wasn't nearly enough to cover his nut. Bardo was a different kind of animal though, Landon knew it when his dad sold his beloved Lowe deck boat one day and returned home with the mare and didn't even get drunk that night, which came as a shock to his fellow swift boat operators. Landon, who was thirteen or fourteen at the time, asked him what he did with the boat and Mr. Briggs said it's in escrow. "Escrow? Is that in California?" Landon asked.

Mr. Briggs was of a mind to turn that horse into a cow. A *cash* cow to be exact. All his life Mr. Briggs had wanted more than anything to raise a champion and, with the prospect of his son becoming one approaching zero, he felt he had to make do with the varmint. But, in the way of easing his son's fear of being replaced, at least as far as paternal attention goes, he did let Landon pick out a proper name for it. "I think it'd bode it well if you gave it a good name," Mr. Briggs explained to Landon. It didn't take Landon, in full puberty at the time, too long to belch with all his raging hormones: "Bardot Hollywood! The 't' is silent."

"There ain't no 't' in Hollywood, dumbass," Mr. Briggs said.

"I meant the one in Bardot, like the actress. Brigitte Bardot. The 't' is silent."

"If it's silent in the surname, why is it not silent in her given name? That don't make much sense to me. You wanna give the horse a good name, a name that shows consistency because, hear me out son, way you name a horse is how you shape its future. And you want a horse to be consistent, consistently fast, consistently first, consistently consistent," Mr. Briggs said.

"Let's just drop the 't' then," Landon said. "Name it Bardo Hollywood."

"Now that's an interesting name, innit?" Mr. Briggs said, "I think I like it. Bardo." And so the name stuck.

Mr. Briggs later explained to Landon that he only owned a piece of the horse, from the eyes to the ears, say, or better yet, from tail, fully extended, to its asshole. The rest belonged to other investors, which is where Bernie came in, who was given a piece of the horse, which part exactly Mr. Briggs never mentioned, in exchange for legal advice whenever needed. As it happened, Bernie's services were required more often than anticipated, as Bardo Hollywood quickly went, on account of her glass bones, from the great hope of the local track circuit to liability to center point in the crossfire of flying lawsuits between its investors. When the dust settled, Mr. Briggs was left with the empty horse stables, while Bernie somehow ended up with the title to Mr. Briggs's deck boat. Needless to say, Mr. Briggs and Bernie became what one would call mortal enemies and, to Landon's knowledge and Bernie's fortune, the two never crossed paths again. Truth be told, Landon couldn't really account for the later years, seeing as he'd left his dad in the lurch when he was but a young buck.

* * *

The musty memories flood back into Landon's mind like the scent of his father's cheap Macho Musk cologne as he stands in front of the decrepit and empty house for the first time in decades. He had just turned sixteen when he left home for good, a day imprinted in his memory like all the other fateful, mostly disastrous, moments in his life. There he was, his teenage self, erect like a statue in the middle of the living room, a duffel bag and a guitar with a yellow "Police Line Do Not Cross" strap resting at his feet. Facing him was his dad, Mr. Briggs, who had on a red flannel shirt and puffed on a cigar as he sat comfortably in a peacock-shaped wicker chair, the lamp on the nearby table bathing him in a red hue. There was a glass of whiskey on the table, well within reach, with a few worn out books by the likes of Céline, Cioran, Henry Miller and other authors whose names meant nothing to the younger Landon, but whose works had caught Mr. Briggs' imagination of late, the books serving as coasters, or rather, companions who Mr. Briggs liked to quote from liberally whether the occasion called for it or not.

Then there came Mr. Briggs' speech, recorded in Landon's selective memory as starting in media res, addressing his son in this manner, more or less:

"… not that you ever gave two shits about her. I don't know what you might've heard through the grapevine, but I put all my chips on Bardo Hollywood and crapped out. Only by some miracle we still have a roof over our heads. What a fuckin' dummy I can be sometimes. There, I said it. Your daddy can be a real dumb sonofabitch when he wants to. That makes you happy, huh, to hear that? Don't just grin and nod, you turd. Know who you remind me of? That asshole Steven Gold. My best friend for thirty years, did everything together, Steven and I, from chasing skirts to gambling to anything you can think of that wasn't free of charge, which is to say the fun things in life."

Landon strained to recall that name but wasn't able to. He knew he was bad with names, couldn't remember people's names to save his life, but still felt like he should've heard Steven Gold mentioned before. It's true, on the other hand, Mr. Briggs did call his friends mostly by nicknames and other such appellations so maybe that's why it never registered with Landon. Maybe he was the one went by Goldibucks, god knows, Landon was always on a strict need-to-know basis with his old man.

"He bankrolled me at first, Steven Gold," Mr. Briggs said, "got me off the ground, and *then* fucked me over. Wasn't for him I woulda never bought that thoroughbred though. Guy was, how you kids say nowadays, *money*. He was money, with a shit-eating grin. Kinda guy always looks like a million bucks. Looks into a mirror and sees Adonis looking back. Motherfucker says to me once, 'You are what you eat, what you wear, what you drive, what you make, and that's it.' Said that with a straight face, like he was telling me some kinda secret to the Universe. The stupid cunt! Don't listen to that nonsense, son, trying to reduce you to nothing. Look beyond a man's bare necessities, you might be surprised. There's a mind, a soul, a consciousness. Not that any o'that ever bothered greaseball Steven Gold. He'd always find his way around the checks and controls, had a way about him where he could grease the cogs in a papier-mâché. Why he got into politics, I guess. Suits his temperament. Never insults no one to their face 'cause he wants their fucking vote. And the more lies he feeds 'em the bigger their heads. 'Cause the little man, he loves to get buttered up, thinks he's special, don't he. Bunch o' jackasses all o'em, with a driver's license and a business card tells 'em who they are. "Every man a king," he says. What the *fuck*! Really? Flatterers oughta be shot, simple as that. World would be a better place without their empty carcasses stinking it up to the high heavens. But I gotta come clean with you here, I too was drunk on Steven Gold's lies until I saw him in the light of day. Day of the accident, day Bardo Hollywood broke her leg, *that* day. I was just breezing her, daily routine, nothing less nothing more, and then it happened. Freak accident, or maybe it was simply meant to happen, I don't know. I put that mare down myself, I felt like she was telling me to grab the syringe from the vet and be a man about it, not let a stranger put her out of her misery. I swear I heard that thought pop into my mind, straight from the horse's *head* to mine. I've no doubt about it, it was her last wish in this life, and I worked up the courage to do it. I pumped the poison in and said a prayer, something I made up on the spot, felt like the right thing to do and watched the life ebb away outta that body, a perfect body but for the one thing, the one thing that broke the whole. And then I wasn't back to the stables for ten minutes, still grieving over the whole damn thing, when a man in a suit pops up outta nowhere, this mousy little guy says he's Steven Gold's lawyer, suing me for negligence. I tried to call my friend, but he wouldn't pick up, wouldn't return my calls, turned his back on me completely. He owned that thoroughbred from the muzzle to the saddle, so to speak, but making his insurance premiums was apparently too much for Steven Gold. No, he complained that seven percent of the mare's value went down the drain every month, he bitched and moaned about it until he let the policy lapse and only way to get his money back was by suing me for intentional harm. He wanted my house and the little money I'd saved up for you. Yeah, I put away some dough thinking one day you might wanna make a man of yourself, settle down, start a family."

The younger Landon had to chuckle at that idea. He had grandiose plans for the future, especially the immediate future, but starting a family didn't feature in there except maybe for something he might take a gander at when he retired from the public stage as a legend, as a way to do the world a favor by continuing his bloodline. But just a few short years later he would fall in love with the woman of his dreams, quite literally, and they would have two children, Jason and Tyler, born eight years apart, and they would settle down like most suburban families, at least for a while, like Mr. Briggs had dreamed, until the event that shook that life to its foundation.

"Wasn't much different with my other partner, Keith Brood," Mr. Briggs continued. "This is a guy I went to school with, enlisted together, served together, wasn't a time I can remember I didn't know Keith Fuckin' Brood. He's my first cousin, as bloodlines go, but really he was my brother. I'm godfather to three of his fuckin' kids, the triplets. In fact, his step-brother Bill married my ex. That is, *your* mother. Which goes to show how things have a way to stay in the family. So now you know, 'case you're wondering about this or that person and how come you weren't kept in the loop about 'em. Reason is you're still a dumb kid who only wants to party and wouldn't understand things way they're meant to be understood. But now you leave me no choice so hear me out, you might even finesse a moral outta this fuckin' story. I go ask Keith Brood, my first-cousin, my brother, my family, my own blood, to help me fight that asshole Steven Gold, and guess what. Says he feels sorry, but he has to watch after his own interests, that he's got four kids to raise, whereas I only got one with one foot out the door anyway, so I got less on the line. Tells me he's already joined Steven Gold in the lawsuit, and would I mind if he came by the house to take some measurements, see what kinda furniture he's gonna need to buy once my house becomes *his*. The nerve on that corrupt monkey. That lazy fuck, infatuated with expensive things, with brute strength, with con men, despising the weak. Now he calls his vices 'virtues'. It's all topsy-turvy, ain't it?"

Now, Keith Brood, he knew. Landon knew him as Uncle Keith, while Mr. Briggs called him Broodsky. Same guy. Once when he was a kid, Landon saw him grab his mom's ass in the kitchen but kept to himself and didn't tell his dad about it for fear of retaliation. He's hated Uncle Keith ever since. Once an asshole, always an asshole.

"Lucky me, I did have one other friend, who shall remain nameless, so as to protect the innocent," Mr. Briggs said. "You wouldn't know her anyway 'cause I've never invited her to the house. I've known her for some time but only casually, I'd run into her at this or that event and chat up a little bit, I introduced her to a few friends of mine from back in the day, I might've sent her a Christmas card once or twice, that sort of thing. To be honest, she's one smart cookie, kinda intimidating to a guy like me. But I knew she hung out amongst lawyers, so I picked up the phone and, boy, was she happy to hear from me. She says to me, "Listen, I know I was never part of your inner circle, but I'll never forget the few times you've shown me kindness and for those moments I intend to pay you back but with interest." Turns out she was a judge herself, little did I know, so she hooked me up with a top lawyer, friend of hers, and she helped me get out of this mess. All pro bono, that's 'free of charge' to you, so I didn't have to pay a dime. All for the few niceties I threw her way over the years. Now that's what I call a true friend. I said to her, "I don't know what to say to you other than, you are a *Goddess*."

Mr. Briggs paused, took a sip of the whiskey, rapped his knuckles on the stack of books and then carried on without mercy, ready to deliver the death blow.

"Which brings me to why I gotta lay it on the line for you, Landon. I know we ain't exactly seen eye to eye in all manner of things, but I'll say my conscience will not be clear if at any point in the future you'll find yourself saying "But my daddy never told me!" Well, young blood, you'll never be able to use that pathetic excuse for an alibi 'cause this is where you daddy tells you like it is. So etch this in that rebellious brain of yours 'cause whenever you'll find yourself in trouble, and trust me you will, I'll be the one hovering over your shoulder, whispering 'Toldya so!" Best of all, I'm gonna lay it all out for you here, free of charge, and I ain't gonna wiggle my tail in an effort to please, I ain't gonna sugar-coat the pill. So hear me out. I ain't no prophet but I seen the world around me enough to know this. You walk outta here today you'll never amount to anything other than a total shit. That's what *they* think of you. Yeah, everybody. That's the plain truth. I mean, if you're lucky… and I mean lucky… and being a

Briggs that's unlikely... there's a sliver of a chance you'll be forgiven for being such a disgusting piece of shit... if only you can hold your chin up like a man in the face of all the sorrows and misfortunes that are sure to come your way in this life, sooner or later. If you're humble, which you're not. If you keep your fuckin' mouth shut, which you don't. If you stay in your seat and do what you're told. Then maybe, but I wouldn't bet on it. It's not forgiveness that's waiting for you out there, son, it's heartbreak and misery."

Mr. Briggs pointed at the guitar on the floor.

"Anyone truly creative, soon as they open their mouth, they're cut down to size by envy. If they're not, then they're false prophets. Now the whole world has become a beehive of mind slaves, and if you don't watch your step you're gonna fall in line like everybody else. Life, you moron, is hemlock on the rocks. Poison's in your bloodstream as we speak, while you lookin' for answers in all the wrong places thinking you look cool with a fucking drink in your hand," Mr. Briggs says, lifting his glass up, "happiness just around the corner. But there ain't no such thing. The poison will take hold of you when you least expect it. Are you ready to become a martyr? Are you ready to bury your loved ones?"

Are you ready to bury your loved ones?

"Save your soul and when you finally shed this mortal coil maybe you'll take one last look back and give a tip of the hat to your old man," Mr. Briggs said.

"I would appreciate that. But watch your step and don't get too worked up about it. That's the most a guy like you can hope for."

Mr. Briggs took a drag of the cigar, then pointed to the duffel bag on the floor.

"Now, with all pleasantries outta the way, this here duffel bag contains all your worldly possessions, which I packed for you as a courtesy. There's your guitar, tuned to four-thirty-two."

He took out a set of keys from his pocket and tossed them at Landon.

"And these are the keys to that piece of shit pickup truck parked in the driveway. It runs pretty good considering. It's yours, a gift from your daddy. You're sixteen, and a grown-up man, in your own words. Now, son, you've just arrived at a fork in the road— you either stay here and do as I tell you, no questions asked, or kindly get the fuck outta my house and go grab the world by the bull horns. Your false idols are awaiting just outside that door."

A moment of silence followed, with Landon standing there motionless like a painter's model. His shirtsleeves were rolled all the way up, rocker style, and there was a raw "Om" symbol tattoo visible on the side of his arm. He'd just gotten that first tattoo on his birthday the week before, a gift from his small posse. They'd all pooled the money and dragged him to a tattoo parlor on Sunset Strip before heading out to a house party in West Hollywood, another sweet sixteen birthday bash. Not his. Actually, Landon didn't even know the host, some rich spoiled girl who'd just put out a pop album and had a book, a memoir no less, coming down the pipeline. Mr. Briggs forbade Landon any kind of extravagance, never mind a birthday celebration, so Landon pretended, in his mind, that he was co-hosting the party, so he quickly made himself at home and took full advantage of the amenities. Around midnight he ended up in the pool and the bandage on his tattoo came off. He poured some whiskey on it later, but it still got infected and swollen to the point of clouding his judgment, such was the mental state he found himself in while facing that particular fork in life's road.

At last Landon reached down, threw the guitar over his shoulder and picked up the duffel bag. He walked to the front door. A soft yellow light trickled in through the small window in the foyer. He hesitated for a moment and thought of his old man living the rest of his days in solitary, whether he'd ever forgive him for walking out on him like this. But when Landon glanced back he realized that his dad, a book open on his lap, had already moved on.

The front door opened and closed with a creak.

Guitar over his shoulder, Landon walked away from his childhood temple and toward the great unknown, his adult life.

* * *

Landon's heart instantly sinks as he takes in the general disrepair and decrepit state of the house. He can hardly believe that anyone was able to live there until recently and couldn't help but feel a tinge of sadness imagining his dad's final days. Even the peacock chair is in the same spot he'd left it, only worn out with age.

"I prefer to remember him the way he used to be, before our friendship ended," Bernie says. He cracks the back door open and leads Landon to the two horse stables in back. "There's termite damage to the horse stalls. And you can hear the bees. Feel free to take a look for yourself."

Landon pokes his head in to assess the damage. Sure enough, a swarm of bees buzz around a beehive hanging in the corner of a stall like a tumor. Bernie only dares to poke his head in. "I heard that he sold his last horse years ago. He was probably using the stables for storage. I don't suppose you own a horse, Landon."

"My son has a pony. He just got it for his birthday. Best present he ever got," Landon says, waiting for a nod of approval. "Ever, ever. *His* words, not mine."

* * *

Landon takes a seat in his dad's peacock chair and drops a dog-eared copy of "The Complete Idiot's Guide to Wills and Testaments" on his lap. Bernie, seated catty-corner from him, pulls out a batch of legal documents, which Landon glances over as if he was familiar with the kind. "When did the testator last amend his will?" Landon asks with a fake-it-till-you-make-it attitude.

"Just a couple of months ago."

"What was the subject of said…" Landon flips through his book. *"Codicil?"*

"To my surprise, he named *me* his will executor," Bernie says. "As you can well imagine, given the circumstances."

"I was as surprised as you. I clearly remember you two having a falling out years ago, over that damn racehorse," Landon says, "Bardo Hollywood."

"I never got the meaning of that name. Your father must have been drunk when he named it," Bernie smiles and smacks his lips, "but then, what do I know about horses. I'm just a humble lawyer. We did have some common friends, your father and I, and I would inquire of him from time to time. I heard that by the end of his life your father had turned into a misanthrope. Turned out, I wasn't the only one he hated. He hated *everybody*."

"When you told me he left me something I was hoping for cash but now I'm beginning to think it's a piece of rope," Landon says, mimicking a hanging.

Bernie doesn't laugh at the joke. He keeps his poker face, expertly circumcises a couple of Cuban cigars and hands one to Landon like a peace offering, which he gladly accepts, happy to take a smoke break from all that legalese.

"Only the best for my friends." They sink deep in their chairs and light up. "Tell me something, Landon," Bernie says, "Have you ever heard of *L'Dor Va'Dor*?"

"I can't say that I have. What's that, a rock band?"

"In my tradition it represents the belief that a father is obligated to do a number of things to help his son become a man," Bernie says.

"Oh, I see."

"A father has to circumcise his son, redeem his son, teach him about our holy book, the Talmud," quickly adding, "or the Torah, if they're so inclined, help him get married, and teach him a craft," Bernie says, holding a finger up for each task he mentions. "And some say, teach him how to swim," he chuckles.

"Interesting."

"There are certain things that a father should do to properly send a son out into the world. You might have something of the sort in your own tradition, I'm sure."

"Dad gave me a lecture before I left the roost, and not much else," Landon says. "But I have that speech imprinted in my memory and every now and then I replay it in my head. Works when I'm up and works when I'm down."

Landon points to the armchair. "As a matter of fact, while he gave me that speech he was sitting in this very chair, like some kind of home-grown Buddha, shooting it straight, mincing no words."

"What sort of things did he speak of?"

"Things about the world and its trappings. At first I thought he was completely nuts, just out-of-his-mind crazy, and mean, too, but after all these years I feel like I'm beginning to understand him more," Landon says, taking a big puff out of his cigar, "even side with him."

"Did he offer you help in a material way?"

"No, he didn't have much himself. All his money went into his horses," Landon says, wistfully. "He wanted to leave a mark on the world, but the task sucked the life out of him."

"I do remember a time when he would starve himself to make sure his horses were well fed," Bernie says. "He bet everything on that one thoroughbred, but he was terribly unlucky with the freak accident. Terribly unlucky."

"Yeah, I guess he never recovered from that," Landon says.

Bernie rests his cigar on an ashtray. "Listen, Landon, you're a smart guy. A little misguided, perhaps, but smart in the ways of the world. When I first came to this town I had nothing. The only person to offer me a helping hand was your old man. He introduced me to some Hollywood types, folks he'd met while strutting his horses on movie sets, and I was eventually able to grow a clientele. I will never forget his act of kindness. And despite our falling out I feel like I owe him a debt of gratitude."

Bernie reaches for a stack of papers, which he hands to Landon. "And I'm only doing this as a way to repay that debt and honor his memory."

Landon gives it the once-over, but it might as well have been written in Chinese. "I don't get it. What's this?"

"There's good news and bad news. The bad news is your old man left you his house," Bernie says, and pauses there to let the news sink in.

"How's that *bad* news?" Landon asks.

"There's a notice on the front door, I don't know if you saw it," Bernie says. "The house is red tagged. Has been since two or three earthquakes ago."

"I don't understand," Landon says.

"There's a quote in there for what the repair costs would be. I'm talking about minimal repair costs to please the city inspectors."

Landon turns to that page. "Man, that's sure a lot of money to just blow some shit up."

"On the next page you'll find a quote for what the land is worth," Bernie says.

"Awright, I get it," Landon says. "So, you're saying he basically bequeathed me a debt."

"I'm afraid so."

"Can't wait to hear the *good* news," Landon says.

Bernie pulls a paper out of the stack and points to a number written on it, as if to say, yeah, that's for real. "Good news is I'm willing to pay you that amount for the house. That way you won't need to worry about anything right now, and I know you're going through a difficult and emotional time, and you can thank me later."

"That's very generous, Bernie."

He's hardly finished the sentence when Bernie already has a checkbook out, pen in hand and ready to shoot like an outlaw out of a Western flick. "You can sign it over to me at your convenience and you'll walk away with less worries and more cash than you've ever seen," Bernie says.

"Let me take a couple of days to review this de facto, uh, pari passu proposal," Landon says, unloading the last legal term he could remember. He surprised himself with that reply. The words came out of his mouth like vomit, he had no control over it. That is, the business about taking his time to review the deed. His more practical mind already had a long list of shit he was gonna buy with that money, wild parties were already unfolding in his head and yet, the words came out with an authority beyond his control, and he just couldn't renege on it.

"That's not what it is… But, yes, of course," Bernie says. If there's a flash of slight disappointment on Bernie's face, Landon couldn't spot it. A bottle of Scotch pops out of Bernie's hands like a rabbit out of a magician's hat. He pours into two glasses, god knows where he has been hiding those.

"Just curious, what happened between you and dad?" Landon asks, just to break the awkward silence if nothing else.

"If you'll excuse me, Landon, I don't wish to speak ill of the dead," Bernie says, and they clinked their glasses. "L'chaim. To life."

"Cheers, man." Landon says, then takes a sip and lets the spirits slowly burn their way down inside his body until he suddenly breaks into a cold sweat that makes him wonder if it's the onset of a panic attack.

"My father had a saying: *A freint darf men zich koifn, sonem kright men umzist,* Bernie says, as he downs his shot.

"Sorry, my pig Latin ain't what it used to be," Landon jokes, wanting more than anything to get out of the house, feeling like he's suffocating in there, like the spirit of his dead father is inhabiting that same space, and the room itself, too small to contain it, is busting out at the seams.

"A friend you have to buy, enemies you get for nothing," Bernie says. "That's in Yiddish."

"Your father didn't speak Hebrew?"

"No. He spoke Yiddish."

"Oh, I just thought..." Landon says, "never mind," and downs his drink to send Bernie a clue that their meeting is over, and the terms have been agreed upon. But to his surprise, Bernie starts to sing a song in Yiddish, or maybe Hebrew, Landon couldn't tell anyway. *"L'Dor Va'Dor, L'Dor Va'Dor, L'Dor Va'Dor nagid god'lecha…*" Bernie sings and sings like a drunk baritone, while Landon shuts his eyes and droops into his dad's chair. He thinks to thank Bernie for finding him and bailing him out of jail earlier in the day, an event Landon registered as very high on a scale of dead certain to miracle but can't quite muster the energy to bring his thoughts into the world.

* * *

The next thing Landon remembers is a loud knock on the door. It takes him a few moments to get his bearings. He's still sitting in the peacock chair, but no Bernie in sight, so he must've been out for some time. He checks the paperwork again to make sure he didn't sign anything while unconscious. Which, given his history, wouldn't come as a complete surprise.

Jesse, a young Native American with a ponytail, drags his Pest Control equipment out onto the back yard. He puts on a yellow protective bee suit before entering the barn where Landon, happy to be out in the open air, is keeping the bees company.

"I hear they stung a pony," Jesse says. "Like two houses over. Found bees in his ears, in his nose. He dead, bro."

"You're shittin me," Landon says.

"I think they're Africanized."

"How can you tell?"

"Way they look, they're just like the others. But these, you can't reason with them, bro." He points at a foam container. "Don't worry, nothing I can't handle." And just as he says that, a bee lands on his hand and puts a stinger in it.

"Sonofabitch," Jesse screams, flapping his arm up and down like he's fighting an invisible enemy. "They're out to get us," he says, as he points his index finger to the beehive like Zeus. "Someone's gonna pay for this!" He picks up his head gear and puts on a red LA Clippers "Griffin" jersey *over* the bee suit. He then steps inside like an astronaut first walking on a hostile planet.

* * *

Landon is back on the old peacock chair when the room starts to shake. He holds in his hands the check for the house, which would cover his debt to the Army and leave him plenty of pocket change. Framed pictures fly off the walls and the whole house rocks back and forth as if the Hand of God placed it on top of a giant wave.

Whether it's an aftershock or an entirely new quake, Landon isn't quite sure, nor is he apparently concerned. His mind is on the deal, and he just can't pull the trigger on either option. Cash the check, get rid of his childhood home and become yet another sucker, much like his dad, on a long list of Briggs males fucked over by lawyers. Or tear the check and inherit, like Bernie said, a debt he can't pay.

Landon remains calm and serene for the entire duration of the temblor. His thoughts are racing in all directions at once. The house makes a noise like all his favorite songs playing at once.

Maybe he is dreaming.

A scene unfolds in Landon's head like it's playing on a screen.

On the other side of the city, Ray checks his watch, then his goons copy his move and collectively shake their heads. Lex helps himself to a bag of chips from the vending machine. "He's not bringing the truck, Ray," Lex says.

"I know," Ray says, "I wonder if he might be going to the Chinaman to fence the cargo."

"That'd be his last mistake. Zhang would eat him alive," Lex says.

"And it's bye-bye cigarettes for us, too."

"Sure as the day is long."

"Someone needs to teach this fool a lesson," Ray says.

"You had to give him the benefit of the doubt, but now he's pissed away that little bit of goodwill."

"That way I won't feel sorry for what I'm about to do to him."

"You need to think in terms of reciprocal justice," Lex says.

"What's that, like an eye for an eye?"

"Yes. You'll have to think what stealing a truck full of cigarettes would be worth in human terms."

"I'm gonna fucking kill him. That's what," Ray says.

"Recover the truck and the cigarettes. *Then* kill him," Lex says. "But you'll have to find him first."

"That's not a problem," Ray says, "He really loves his little boy. He can't stay away from him for too long."

"And the mother?"

"Oh, I won't be taking the boy," Ray says. "I'll just borrow him for a little while."

* * *

Leftovers on the kitchen table, soiled dishes in the sink. The TV is on in the living room. Some redneck is about to break a chair over his wife's ex-boyfriend's cousin's head . No one is watching. Landon and Stephanie are in the bedroom down the hallway, naked and sweaty under the sheets. Landon stares at the ceiling. Stephanie wraps her arm around Landon. He twitches slightly at this intrusion.

"What's going on with all these earthquakes? That was a pretty strong one even earlier today. You feel that?" Landon asks.

"What time did it hit?" she asks.

"Around noon. I was at my dad's house, thought the ceiling would crash down on me."

"Oh. I must've been napping," Stephanie says.

"Noon too early for you?"

"Can't sleep at night. Nightmares." She shifts in her spot, braces herself for a big reveal. "I'm changing my name."

"What's wrong with Stephanie?" Landon asks.

"No, dummy, my roller derby name, Barbie Drone. I don't like it any more."

"Why?"

"I feel like I've outgrown it."

"What're you gonna change it to?"

"Well, I had this strange dream last night," Stephanie says. "I was being attacked by a Barbie Doll."

"Oh, no."

"But it wasn't your run of the mill Barbie, it had four arms, sharp teeth, her tongue was sticking out, she had skulls in her hair, blood was dripping down her chest, it was frightening," Stephanie says. "So I told the girls about it this morning and they said it was Kali, the Hindu goddess of Death and Liberator of Souls."

"Whoa."

"Yeah, so I took that as a sign," she says. "I'm gonna change my name to Kalibrate. Spelled with a K."

"Mmmm-K…"

"So what do you think?" Stephanie says, as she moves closer to him, stroking his cheek.

"Sounds good. Do what you gotta do, y'know." Landon removes Stephanie's arm from his chest and slips out of the bed, stepping over some Barbie dolls. She turns over with a huff.

"You were in my dream, too," she says, but he's oblivious to all that drama. Landon walks over to the living room and opens the balcony to a fourth-floor panoramic view of downtown. Some kind of art walk is happening down below. His head looks like it's immersed into a sea of neon lights.

Landon is a casual smoker but when he spots one of Stephanie's packs of cigarettes on the floor of the balcony next to a lighter, he can't resist billowing some smoke into the L.A. air in memory of his dead father, much like his army buddies pouring libations in memory of their fallen brothers. He lights up and looks down to spot a teenage boy, about Jason's age as frozen in Landon's mind, running down the street with his dog. It's a large dog, too, a Labrador perhaps, and next to the boy it appears as big as a pony. The dog stops to pee and the boy looks up straight at Landon and holds his gaze. The resemblance between the two boys is striking, the same lanky silhouette and wavy brown hair, the same gait, the same pointy chin and sad eyes. Under different circumstances, Landon feels like he wouldn't have thought twice before calling out to him by his name, *Jason*. But what is he to make of all this now?

Are you ready to bury your loved ones?

Mr. Briggs' line echoed in Landon's head one day, some years ago, while sitting in a doctor's office at Children's Hospital LA on a beautiful Friday morning. The Tuesday prior he jumped out of bed just after ten a.m. (after a closing shift at the Good Luck Bar), as if awakened by a nightmare, though strangely he couldn't remember having dreamed at all. He was washing his face when the phone rang. It was the principal from Jason's elementary school, telling him that his kid had fainted during second grade P.E., probably dehydrated, and wouldn't he come pick him up early. Landon found him waiting in the Nurse's office, bottle of water in his hand. He took one look at the boy, and he felt it in his heart that it was something serious.

The doctor, holding the ECG results, only confirmed to Landon what he already knew. The boy's heart was suffering. Long QT syndrome, he called it. Electrical disturbance in the workings of the heart. Look at the twisted waves on this ECG, the doc said, the lower chambers of the heart are going berserk. Torsades de Pointes, the doc called it. English, please, said Landon. *Twisting of the points*. It lasts more than a minute it leads to fainting, then full-body seizure, then Death. How long, Landon asked. There's medication, the good doctor said, but who's to say, could be a year from now, could be twenty years. The doc was in the ballpark. It was seven years later that Landon buried his son and despite the heads-up he was never ready for it.

Landon puts out his cigarette on the rail of the balcony. The dog soon finishes its business and jumps ahead of the boy, showing him the way back home. Landon tries to ascribe a reason for all the build-up inside his emotional buttress dam but has to give up that pursuit when he figures reason has nothing to do with it.

Landon peeks back inside to make sure Stephanie hasn't caught him in this volatile emotional state. Once assured that no one is watching he turns his attention back to the action down the street and is startled to see, in the very spot that the boy and his dog have just vacated, the Traveler. He stands there on the sidewalk, holding tight to his suitcase, staring straight ahead at the boy and his dog. He doesn't look up to Landon and doesn't need to. A message is being sent that both understand without a need to elaborate.

At last, Landon wipes his face and steps inside, turning his back to a neon lit backdrop that changes throughout the long night in a rhythm that might appear, at first glance, chaotic and random, but which belongs in fact to a higher order, one that effortlessly sets the score straight between the past and the future.

*"There's no difference
    between
          love
  and
hate."*

The Tibetan Book of the Dead, Day Five

Trucks of all sizes are strewn throughout the chain-link fenced lot like carcasses in an elephant cemetery. Some are being taken apart limb by limb, others are being breathed new life into, as with all things in Nature's playground. "Which one is ours?" Frankie asks, peeking over the steering wheel, parked as they are across the chop shop's main office.

"I don't know," Landon says, "must be hidden in plain sight."

Cassidy, dressed in a green track suit, steps out of his office accompanied by his ten-year-old sons, Sal and Val, twins for all to see. There are Halloween decorations everywhere and a sign on the wall reads *"God we trust. Everyone else pay cash!"*, flanked by two giant plastic spiders. Cassidy walks over to a mechanic and, after exchanging a few words, he turns to his son Val, who promptly sticks his right arm out to the side. Cassidy blurts out a barrage of questions about a catalytic converter, all the while pressing down with two fingers on Val's wrist until the boy's arm eventually goes down.

"Are they fuckin' stupid?" Frankie asks.

"No, man, it's like he's using an oracle," Landon says.

"A *what*?"

"An oracle, like he's divining the future," Landon says.

"Oh, you mean like gypsy fortune telling, like coffee reading, that kinda shit?"

"Something like that."

"The oracle, that would be the kid, right?" Frankie says, then takes a long look at Landon as if to make sure he's not being punked.

"Yeah. He explained it to me the other day," Landon says, "it's this technique based on the nature of consciousness. Like at our higher levels we're aware of the truth and even though we don't know it consciously, the body, like a good soldier, responds to the high command. You follow?"

The oracle's arm keeps going down at the slightest touch, further exacerbating Frankie's confusion. "What the fuck does that have to do with the kid signaling for low dip?" Frankie asks.

"Some folks have this gift," Landon says, "when they hear the truth their bodies trigger an involuntary reflex. Say, you ask the kid, does the Sun rise in the east, kid's arm goes down when you apply a little pressure to it. You ask him something obviously false like, has Landon Briggs been a responsible adult, his arm will be stiff as rigor mortis."

"Oh, oh," says Frankie, now fully enlightened to the phenomenon, "it's like that Cherokee dude, what's his name, guy used to go around dowsing for water and shit. Had like a Y-shaped tree branch."

"Sherman Silko," Landon says.

"That's right! Sherman fuckin' Silko," Frankie says.

"Feather of the Wide Mountain, by his traditional name."

"Semper fi, motherfucker."

"He had a gift."

"Don't know about that," Frankie says, "I mean he went looking for water on account he wanted to drink it straight from the source, some kind an Injun ritual I believe, and found himself a goddamn land mine. The thing popped three times. Boom-boom-boom-boom! The gift that kept on giving."

"That's true," Landon says, "But you're forgetting the land mine was smack on top of a water source."

"What water? Dude got blown up to fine sand."

"He did get blown up, but he would've survived the injuries, minus a leg or two, if not for the water. Came out like a goddamn geyser. He flew up a distance then landed face down in a big puddle of water, man," Landon says. "They couldn't get to him fast enough for fear of landmines. In the meantime, Sherman Silko was busy drowning."

"He shoulda first dowsed for landmines, huh," Frankie says.

"He didn't know there were landmines down there. He knew there was water, so he went looking for what he knew was there," Landon says.

"I think maybe there's a moral to this story, don't you think?" Frankie says. "Like somewhere in there."

"And what would that be?"

"Oh, I don't know, like you can't quench your thirst if you're dead," Frankie says, and shakes his head up and down proudly, impressed with his profound statement. "I oughta put that on T-shirts."

"So you're saying Sherman Silko turned into an ever-thirsty ghost?"

"You best believe it."

"Now there's a movie I'd like to see, The Legend of Sherman Silko: The Ever-Thirsty Ghost," Landon says, before stepping out of the car to greet Cassidy and the twins. A guard dog snarls at Frankie but Cassidy yells at it in a foreign tongue, only its name, Cerberus, registering with Landon out of the deluge of consonants, and the dog whimpers away still undefeated.

"Follow me, guys," Cassidy says, and leads the pack to the back of the lot, his twin boys flanking the grownups like miniature bodyguards. Cassidy peels a removable decal off the door to a truck, to reveal Ray Barba's truck company logo underneath.

"Nice. So how much longer can we keep the truck here?" Landon asks.

"Well, let's see," Cassidy says, and he turns to face Val, who juts his arm out to the side just like before. Cassidy raises his eyes and keeps them there for a few quiet moments. Frankie follows his gaze and cups his hand over his eyes whereupon he spots an airplane and points at it like he's never seen such a thing. At last, Cassidy takes a deep breath and shoots his question into the deep void, "Is it safe to keep this truck on the lot for more than a week?" Cassidy gently tries to push Val's arm downward, but it wouldn't budge. The deep void has spoken.

"More than five days?" Cassidy follows up. The deep void, by means of Val's stiff arm, again shouts... no way, Jose.

"More than two days?" Nope.

"For one more day?" Finally, the boy's arm lowers to his side, and Cassidy beams the oracle's sanction to Landon and Frankie. "There you have it. Two days tops," he says.

"Jeezuz, I hope we're not all dead by then," Landon says. He produces a wad of cash and pays Cassidy for his trouble. In turn, Cassidy hands him a set of keys, with a business card inserted in the key ring. "This key is for front gate, case you need access at night. This other one is for lock I put on trailer, and this here is for new ignition," Cassidy says.

Landon sneaks a peek in the back of the truck to make sure the cargo's still there. It is. "I've been meaning to ask you, Cassidy, you mind if I try this thing you're doing, this divination?"

"Sure, man," Cassidy says, busy now counting his cash. Landon turns to Sal, says "Stick your arm out, kid." Cassidy looks up for a second, his fingers still fully engaged. "Oh, it don't work on Sal," he says.

"Why not?"

"He's a goddamn *atheist*," Cassidy says, and shakes his head, taking parental responsibility for this sad state of affairs. The boy, Sal, simply shrugs, like "hey, what can I tell you guys, it is my ethos and my hard-earned belief and I'm sticking with it." Cassidy goes on to explain, "*Val* is oracle boy, he is on different level that boy. This other one, he insulted the gods," and he promptly smacks Sal upside the head.

Val sticks his right arm out, ready to entreat the gods. Landon takes his time composing his inquiry. "Will I get my wife and kid back by the end of the month?" Landon asks, as he presses down on Val's arm. He puts a little elbow grease in it, but the thing won't budge.

"End of the year?" Forget it. Landon kneels down, brings his eyes level with the querent's. "Okay, let's be conservative here. By the end of *next* year?"

Val's arm is still stiff as a log.

Landon and Val appear to be engaged in a staring contest, or otherwise partaking in some sort of nonverbal communication, sizing each other up like prizefighters at weigh-in. "You may be asking the wrong questions, mister," Val says, and he gently caresses Landon's face, the way only a mother would, and it seems to Landon that the moment stretches out forever and the boy's blue eyes open into a clear azure sky in a realm where all the answers are to be found, the meaning of his existence and suffering on this earth, and he reaches in there, Landon does, and demands to be taken to the King's palace and figures it shouldn't be a problem given the legit nature of his grievances but there is only one gate leading into the palatial grounds and the gatekeeper is on high alert, vigilantly patrolling the path girdling around the castle, not a hole to be found in the ramparts, no crack big enough to sneak through, and at the sight of Landon the gatekeeper draws his mighty weapon and says to him that no strangers are allowed in who do not carry the signs on them, and Landon takes that as a clue to shed his clothes and proceeds to spiral around like a ballet dancer for the gatekeeper to check out all the fly signs and symbols tattooed on his mortal body but the gatekeeper is not at all impressed with the impromptu show and exhorts Landon to best return to where he came from, lest he get his head bludgeoned into pulp, and Landon feels the sudden pangs of shame and humiliation at being sized up by eyes that probe past the surface of the skin and into his innermost crevices, exposing what he didn't know was there, and upon having found himself lacking in all the major and minor virtues, insofar as he can ascertain in this altered state, the spell is suddenly broken as Sal blurts out "*He's faking it*," and Val's eyes close and stay closed until Landon is back in the car and on his way back to the city for more of the stuff that brought him there in the first place. So much for consulting the auspices.

* * *

The ride back into the city is getting on Landon's nerves, his head caught squarely in the vice of heavy traffic and Frankie's nonstop bitching about needing to get rid of the evidence before the oracle's deadline.

"That fuckin' kid freaked me out, man," Frankie says. "I ain't about to step on his pronouncements. Lemme tell you somethin', once we're done with this shit I'mna go back there and beg Cassidy to lemme hang out with baby Jesus. Lemme bask in his aura, know what I mean? Maybe start a cult or something. Always good to be an early adopter, right? Just gotta find a buyer for that shit in back of the truck before we can get back to our lives… And dump the truck… Or sell it if we can, don't make no difference to me… what're you thinking, Landon?"

"I say we go to the Chinaman," Landon says.

"Well, shit, I'm gonna need to sleep on that. Last I brought it up I just wanted to see you squirm, wasn't actually considering it as a possibility," Frankie says. "I still got business to take care of in TJ, know what I mean? Won't do if I leave my bones in L.A.," Frankie says.

"You got until tomorrow to find us another buyer then," Landon says. "Else, we're going to the Chinaman."

"That makes me nervous, man. The guy's a stone-cold killer is what I heard. Rumor has it he chopped a dude in half over a gambling debt. Like in the parking lot he did that. We go to his place there's just the two of us standing between him and a million dollars. I've faced worse odds than that and come out smelling like a rose, but I think we oughta hedge our bets here. Know what I'm saying?" Frankie says.

"How big the debt?"

"Huh?"

"You said the Chinaman killed a dude over a gambling debt," Landon says. "How big the debt?"

"I don't fuckin' know, man," Frankie says. "A jade fuckin' turtle, for all I care. That ain't the point. The point is the man's a cold-blooded killer with a well-trained posse who wouldn't think twice before running us through the noodle machine if he caught the slightest whiff that we're disposable. Which we are."

"We can test him out first," Landon says. "Try to unload a small batch, see if he bites, and if all goes well dump the rest of the enchilada later."

"Sounds like a plan. We do that tomorrow?" Frankie says.

"Yeah, I'm gonna set up a meet," Landon says.

"You think I might get away with some concealed weaponry?

"Doubt it. They'll frisk us," Landon says. "We'll be sitting there like lambs before slaughter, I'm telling you. But we got no choice, do we?"

"There's no going back now," Frankie says.

Landon has to agree with that, as he sees himself firmly on a path that doesn't go within a mile of his returning the truck to its owner. The mere idea of doing something that weak almost brings a snicker out of him but he stifles it at the last moment, not wanting to appear too cocky, lest an unexpected turn of events would later give him a good kick in the ass. It was written that the meek shall inherit the earth, but Landon later learned that 'meek' was just a mistranslation of the Greek word 'praus', used to describe trained warhorses. The Greek army would round up wild horses and after months of grueling training some of the animals would perish, some would be discarded, some would be turned into beasts of burden, but a select few were chosen to be warhorses. Facing certain death, these warhorses would charge on a war cry, stop on a whisper. They were then in a state of 'praus', meaning power under authority, nature under discipline, strength under control. Now that's something Landon can roll with. Generally speaking, he keeps to himself when the situation calls for it, praus embodied, and just stares vacantly out the window to avoid conversation. He sees the city as unfolding like a red carpet in front of him, a million faces watching him under the spotlight, each angling for a better view, judging his every step like it was worth a thousand headlines, but out of all the faces soon only the eyes remain and each eye shifts ever so slightly, as if searching for a place to nest, and the lights dim and the red carpet turns into a battlefield and he realizes that each eye is actually inside the pores of a large skin, the skin of a giant that reaches to the Moon and beyond, and

Landon feels a shiver running down his spine and wonders exactly how large this battlefield is and what cosmic lives are riding on his every move.

Which reminds Landon, later that afternoon, as he rushes Tyler out of Melanie's apartment and toward an impromptu rendezvous with the beleaguered pony, *where in the world is Ray fuckin' Barba?* For all he knows, Ray could be hiding in a tinted-windowed car watching his every move like the devil in mufti. Landon does spot a black Escalade down the street, a car much like the one he's seen Ray drive on occasion, and a tingle runs up his spine. It's that old feeling again, his fears materializing into the world with astonishing accuracy or otherwise Landon's ability to sense danger like it's a thriller playing out on a big screen in high-def and Dolby surround sound, but it runs at odds with Landon's rational side, so he pleads ignorance, as per usual, until proven right.

As it plays out, Ray spots them from half a block away. "Fuck, he's got his fuckin' kid with him!" Ray says to his driver. Landon is in disguise somewhat, has on a pair of sunglasses and a wool hat, the kind hipsters wear in the middle of a scalding Cali summer day, presumably to prevent their hair from catching on fire, but even so he's easy to spot, seeing as Tyler's made no attempt at wearing a disguise himself. It's nigh impossible to get the boy to wear a costume even on Halloween, never mind for an off-season occasion. If he's not comfortable with his get-up he won't be dragged out of the house if the house were on fire, and on this day he felt like wearing a wool vest, pink shirt and a blue bow tie, which is to say he's driving Landon fuckin' nuts. Completely unlike his brother Jason, on the other hand, who would throw a ratty old T-shirt on and still feel and look like a rock star in the making. Landon missed that rapport and sometimes couldn't help getting frustrated with his younger son. In fact, for years Landon still had in his possession a bagful of Jason's dirty laundry, which he initially kept under his bed, hoping it would bring about the psychic influence — a mere dream would've sufficed — which connected them while Jason was still alive, but after some time it became clear to Landon that the link was broken and that his son had moved on to other realms where, Landon reckoned, he was sealed off from this world for his own good, as to not get contaminated. After a couple years Landon moved Jason's dirty laundry into a storage facility, along with other artifacts and sentimental by-products of his recent divorce, and when one day he passed by for his bi-monthly routine inspection and discovered his belongings strewn about and nearly completely chewed up by rats and other vermin he collapsed to the floor and cried like at his son's funeral, having to say his good-byes all over again. The following day he cleaned up the storage room and threw away everything in it, damaged or not, and when he got home he took a bath so hot he couldn't see the end of his fingers for the steam and came to the temporary conclusion that whatever sorrows befall him in life, they all happen in a tiny universe that no one really knows or cares about. He felt the sudden urge to be near a warm body and he ended up calling a high-end hooker, the eight hundred per trick variety, but she charged him only six hundred on account of being a repeat customer, and under the guise of vague familiarity he proceeded to spill out all his secrets to her, amongst other things, though he might as well have been talking to a wall. The physical act itself was merely an afterthought and as she left, she told him "I love your cock," and at the time he actually believed her and temporarily forgot about all his troubles.

"Follow them," Ray says to the driver, who gets the SUV rolling and promptly rolls a Stop sign, nearly clipping the rear bumper of a car traversing the intersection.

"Watch the road, will'ya!" Ray yells, his patience being tested yet again by a guy whose only qualification is to be his half-sister's second cousin. The driver's older brothers have already achieved a certain notoriety in criminal circles as harbingers of Death and are in high demand and only accept select hit jobs worthy of their reputation. Few people know their real names, as on the street they go simply by The Diadora Brothers, on account of their habit of donning similar Diadora track suits and shoes while on the job. Ray's driver and the Diadora brothers are in fact part of a famed quintuple birth, something even the local papers in Sicily covered back then as nothing short of a miracle, the story going that the first four baby boys had already been out and practically baptized by the time the last of the litter slinked out of the tunnel to join the world. The first four of the boys went on, as the Diadora brothers, to achieve incredible physical and mental skills in the areas of martial arts and all manner of mortal combat, while the youngest of the bunch would forever be rightfully known as the Runt.

"Sorry. It's just hard to keep track of two things at the same time," the Runt says, which is also the excuse he used to explain how he let Landon get away a couple days earlier.

"What two things?" Ray blurts out.

"Watching the road, that's one…" he trails off while negotiating a turn into zero traffic.

"And two?"

"And two, *driving* on the road," the Runt says, holding two chubby fingers up.

Ray thinks for a moment he might be joking, but no. "You left out talking," Ray says, his mind sorting through a selection of near-future timelines that all end up with the Runt face down in the dirt.

"That's just what I mean. Hard to concentrate under these conditions," the Runt says. Ray reaches into the glove compartment and pulls out a shiny silver Beretta, makes sure there's a round in the chamber. "When they come to a stop in a quiet part of town you cut 'em off. I climb out and take care of Landon, while you wait for me in the car. Am I coming through?"

"Yes, boss. I know," he says.

"Just stop talking, will'ya," Ray says.

"Sure thing, boss."

Landon removes his hat and sets the air conditioner to blast. "There's a trail nearby, where you can ride your horsey," he says to Tyler. He glances in the rearview mirror to check the traffic behind him, doesn't see the Escalade but instead catches a giddy look on his son's face as he shifts in the booster seat.

"I really miss my pony," Tyler says. "I wonder if Agamemnon still remembers me."

"Who? Oh, yeah, yeah, of course he remembers you. I grew up around horses and let me tell you, son, horses never forget their human friends, even after years of separation. He'll remember you as well, I'm sure of that. You were nice to him," Landon says and turns to look at the boy, "Horses are forgiving creatures, but they never forget."

The boy nods. "I asked the pony to come to me in a dream, but he didn't."

"Wait, now, Tyler. You can't just will a horse into your dreams. That's not how it works. Dreams have their own logic."

"But, Dad," Tyler says, near to tears, "I haven't had a dream since the day Jason died." He's bawling his little eyes out now, rocking back and forth in the booster seat. "Why can't I dream like everybody else?"

Landon reaches out to him with his right hand, all the while keeping an eye on the road, but the boy would not relent. "Listen, Tyler, I'm sure you have dreams, you just can't remember them."

"Why can't I remember them?" the boy implores.

"Maybe they're not that important, you know? If it was something you had to know, I'm sure you'd wake up with a good recollection of it," Landon says. "Look at me, I haven't had a meaningful dream in years, either."

"When was the last time you had a good dream?" Tyler asks.

"Many years ago, before I met your mother, and you wanna know something?"

"What?"

"If not for that dream, you wouldn't be alive today," Landon says.

"Tell me it," Tyler says, "and I'll stop crying."

"Okay… well, it was a strange dream, I call it the Dream of the Clock Tower."

"Does it take place in a clock tower?" Tyler asks.

"No, it begins with a Snow Globe resting on a wooden table in the middle of a room. There's a miniature Wooden House inside the Snow Globe. Can you picture it?"

"Yes."

"We hear the sound of the wind whistling and blowing hard against the walls of the country house. The wind chimes jingle. The front door rattles. It opens and then closes with a bang!" Landon slaps his hands hard, startling Tyler. "Can you hear it?"

"I can hear it," the boy says. "What does mi-na-ture mean?"

"It means a smaller version of something," Landon says. "But look, Tyler, you can't interrupt me every ten seconds to ask me what every word means, just try to figure it out from the context—"

"What does con-tex mean?" Tyler asks.

"Here you go again. Means try to figure it out from what came before and what follows, or else I'll never finish the damn story. Understand?"

"Yes, Dad."

"Okay, so we move past the Snow Globe and toward the door leading up to the front porch. Through the crack in the door we get a glimpse of a couple standing just outside the Wooden House, their backs to us. A Man and a Woman stand in front of their house, which looks uncannily like the miniature Wooden House inside the Snow Globe. The Wooden House rests at the bottom of a Green Valley, surrounded by green pastures, everything looks picture perfect. *Arcadian*. The Man and the Woman are both young, in their twenties. They both wear antiquated peasant clothing, with leather skull caps, belonging to another time and place. They hold hands in a rigid posture. Their eyes shift slightly and in unison toward a dark cloud formation that's appeared in the blue sky. The Man raises his left arm and points in that direction. He says, *The Big Storm is coming*."

Landon speaks the words in a slow, deliberate cadence, modifying his voice to fit the characters, making it sound like the words have traveled through the ages, the arduous journey having altered them down to their very essence.

The Woman says, "It was foretold. The waters will flood this Green Valley for a long time to come." Worried, the Man turns to the Woman and says, "You must leave at once. The Storm is fast approaching. You will seek shelter in the City."

"And you?" the Woman asks.

"There is something I need to do before I leave," he says. They walk inside, and the Woman starts to pack, shoves some clothes inside a burlap bag, then she carefully places the Snow Globe on a soft cloth, wraps it, and stuffs it in her bag. She's ready to leave now, and it's time to say goodbye. The Man grabs the Woman in his arms and kisses her like it's for the last time.

"I won't be far behind," he says. "I will meet you at the old Clock Tower." The Woman nods, covers her head with a hood and is on her way just as the wind buffets a window right off its hinges. The sky is low and threatening and has opened up like an upside-down ocean. The Woman scurries down a beaten path when she stops and takes one look behind before vanishing into the woods.

Landon stops at a traffic light on Lankershim. He's gotten so carried away with the story he's forgotten all about that suspicious Escalade. Ray instructs the Runt to keep his distance. "I know where they're going," Ray says. "See that damn pony." The Runt hands him his cell phone. "Enter the name of the place in this app, boss," he says, "in case we lose 'em."

Landon continues, Tyler already hooked by the story, "Meanwhile, our Man is inside a woodshed, his face sweaty, as he fumbles for something in the dark. He stops and smiles when he finds what he was looking for. The Man digs a shovel into the ground in front of the porch. He's already dug a good two feet into the soft soil. He looks up at the sky. The rain is coming down hard now and he's drenched. He leans down and takes another Snow Globe out of its wrapping. He wipes it gently. This Snow Globe looks identical to the one the Woman had taken with her."

"Like a copy of it?" Tyler asks.

"Yeah, like a copy, a duplicate, a twin Snow Globe," Landon says, "which the Man places at the bottom of the pit, careful not to break it. He then proceeds to bury it."

As night falls, Landon continues, the Woman finds herself in front of the gates marking the entrance to an imposing city. She knocks and a narrow slit in the gate opens presently. Two beady eyes peer out, then the gate opens with a creak. The Woman steps inside the City. She looks around but sees no one. The gate closes behind her, no gatekeeper in sight. She walks down a cobblestone street. The only sound is that of her footsteps. Suddenly there's a frantic rush behind her, like the charge of an infantry battalion. She turns, but too late. A masked thief has already snatched her bag containing all her worldly possessions, including the Snow Globe, and vanished like a ghost.

The Woman wanders the city streets, sad that she lost her most precious possessions. She looks completely out of place next to the city folk. She stares down, intimidated by the big stone structures. She turns a corner and finds herself in front of the old Clock Tower. She picks out a spot at the base of the Clock Tower and sits down, exhausted and dejected, as the city folk pass by her in a blur. She closes her eyes and all she hears is the movement of the hands of the Clock Tower, the intricate mechanism housed inside like a brain made out of wheels and cogs and levers and springs. The hands of Time turn faster and faster. Day turns into dusk, as our Woman waits still, her posture stoic and unchanged. She looks in the distance at a dark cloud formation and thinks of her Man.

"What do you think our Man is up to?" Landon asks.

"Is he still burying that Snow Globe?" asked Tyler.

"Oh, he's finished that. The Man now follows the path into the woods, just like the Woman before him. He rushes down the slushy road, but the wind has picked up and he can barely hold his ground."

At last, the Man arrives in the City, just like the Woman before him, and finds himself in a seedy area, a bad neighborhood. The city hoodlums are out in numbers, and they all beckon him from behind red lights and dark corners. Drug addicts, criminals, women of questionable morals, you name it. The Man tries to mind his own business, but he sticks out like a sore thumb, and he soon draws the attention of two young thugs. The thugs look at each other and motion at this strange-looking Man. They wait until the Man turns down a dark alley when they rush him from behind and topple him. They hit him and kick him to the ground until he's barely conscious. The thugs laugh as they go through the Man's pockets, finding nothing. He lies there like a beaten stray dog and thinks of home.

Giant waves roll over the crest of the mountains and pour violently into the valley where his Wooden House now rests unguarded. The whole valley quickly fills up with water, giving birth to a lake, and as the waves break and the water clears, something becomes visible at the bottom of the lake. A house. It looks just like a house inside the Snow Globe. The Wooden House.

"What's the Woman doing now?" Tyler asks.

"The Hands of Time turn and turn on the old Clock Tower, waiting for no one," Landon continues. "The Woman looks up at the Clock Tower. She circles around its base. She shivers with cold, as winter has already come to this land. She heads down a deserted street and finds an Inn to get some food and rest."

"What's an inn?"

"Like a Motel 6, remember the one in Big Bear? But without all the luxuries."

"But wasn't she supposed to wait for the Man?" Tyler asks.

"She waited and waited until she couldn't take it anymore," Landon continues. "Winter came and the Man hadn't arrived yet. Tough to live on the streets when it's freezing cold."

"But what was taking the Man so long?"

"I don't know, Tyler, it's a dream. Time flows differently in a dream, there's no rhyme or reason. Anyway, at last, the Man approaches the Clock Tower. He has a bruise on his forehead and a black eye. He circles around the Clock Tower, looking for the Woman, but there's no one there. He looks up at the Clock, whose hands are turning, now faster, now slower. The Man heads down a deserted street. He stops in front of an Inn and hangs his hat in there. It's daytime now. The Woman watches the news on TV, scenes of a terrible hurricane and its aftermath. Houses blown to smithereens, floods, levies breaking, the works. The Woman cries."

To make the scene reading more dramatic, Landon squirts some water on the windshield and turns the wipers on. He steps on the gas to gobble up the empty length of the road in front of him. Tyler says, "Whoa, Daddy!"

Ray leans to the side, tries to spot Landon's car ahead but sees nothing for half a mile. "We lose 'em, or what?" he asks the Runt. The Runt points at the app, "Oh, I haven't been following them, but we're taking the side streets to avoid traffic. Quickest route there, boss, we'll beat 'em to it." Ray shakes his head, brandishes his handgun like it's a lasso. "Get back on the main road and tail them, moron, like I toldya," Ray screams. "When they get to a quiet street, cut 'em off. When they stop I'll take over. Now get back on Magnolia before I paint this car with your fuckin' brains."

Landon carries on, "In a different part of town, the Man is fast asleep. His hands are crossed over his chest, as if he were dead."

Days have passed by now, maybe months, years. The Woman strolls by the old Clock Tower. She now wears a flowery dress and flat shoes, not quite stylish but more in tune with the city garb. She walks up and down, looking around, dejected. She doesn't remember what she's supposed to be looking for any more. She's just going through the motions, with only a vague memory of what brought her there in the first place. And so it goes, day turns into night, turns into day, night, day… The Woman walks by the Clock Tower again, but only gives it a glance. She is now dressed entirely like a city dweller, dress cut short, high heels, and only remembers her past as if it were a dream. She heads down a bustling city street when a Dandy passes by her, and she catches his eye. He's a young man, dressed very fashionably in a suit, tie, hat, oxford shoes. The Dandy smiles at her and she averts her eyes. The Dandy is not about to give up without a fight, though. He circles the Woman, doffing his top hat. The Dandy points to a Café. I just want a minute of your time, he says. The Woman smiles, coquettishly. The Dandy opens the door to the Café and the Woman follows him inside.

Back at the other inn, our Man lies on the bed in the same position, arms crossed over his chest, like a dead man lying in state. His eyes wide open. He sits up on the edge of the bed. He appears dazed and confused. He parts the drapes and peers outside. He shields his eyes as the light hits him. He spots the Clock Tower in the distance. A shiver runs through him, like hearing the opening chords of an old familiar song. He keeps staring at the moving hands on the Clock Tower, unable to place the nature of his longing.

Meanwhile, the Dandy's making a move on the Woman, trying to impress her with his magic tricks. It appears to be working. The Woman smiles and takes a sip of her drink. She's having a good time. "I see you every day, staring at the old Clock Tower," the Dandy says.

"There's something about it," she says, "I just don't know what…"

"It makes me jealous," the Dandy says, to lighten up the spirits, but the Woman's mood has already turned sour.

"Is she thinking of her Man?" Tyler asks.

"Naw, and the Man ain't thinking of her either. He spots a Temptress on a park bench. A fine-looking woman, all right? She cries and dabs her eyes with a handkerchief. The Man plucks out a flower from a nearby garden and hands it to her. The Temptress smiles. You see, they were just crocodile tears. The Man walks away, but the Temptress catches up with him. She grabs his arm, and they now walk side by side through the City. They're a couple now and, arm in arm, they stroll by the Café. Know which one?" Landon asks his son.

"The one the Woman and the Dandy went into?" Tyler says.

"Correct! Good to see you're paying attention," Landon says. "So, yeah, the Woman and that fucker step out of the Café, holding hands, just as the Man and the Temptress turn a corner, not that they would've recognized each other anyway because, you see, the Hands of Time are turning faster now, they're picking up speed, but no one notices. As the Hands of Time turn faster so does the motion of the planets, of the stars, like the heart of the Universe itself beats faster and faster and to the man on the street everything appears as it always has been, but it *feels* different."

"Like a dream," Tyler says.

"Exactly like a dream, like you know something, but you don't know *how* you know it. You just feel it. And so did the Man and the Woman in my dream, they knew deep down that something was amiss, but they couldn't quite place it, so they just went about their daily routine, doing things that men and women are supposed to do. The Man, still dressed in his street clothing, lies down in bed. The Temptress, wearing only some lingerie, lays down next to the Man and they kiss."

"Do they make babies?" Tyler asks.

"Don't know about that, but way I remember it, it sure looked like they were going for it. Not that our Woman is any less guilty, as she lies in the Dandy's bed, naked under the sheets, while he crawls up next to her."

"Do they kiss, too?"

"They sure do, Tyler, they sure do," Landon says. "It's morning now, and years have passed like the blink of an eye. The Woman's in the bathroom and she runs some water over her face. She raises her head to look at herself in the mirror. She has a black eye, and she looks disheveled. The Dandy screams from somewhere inside the house. Not a pleasant scene, and the more I tried to will my dream self to see what the problem was, the more the scene faded away from me until I saw only a creamy fog and heard nothing but the ticks of a clock. Tick-tock... tick-tock...tick-tock... then when the images came back into focus it was nighttime and I saw the Dandy shoving the Woman out of his house and into the cold, damp street."

Traffic has picked up ahead of them, slowing down to a crawl. Landon honks to squeeze himself between two cars.

"Is the Woman homeless now?" Tyler asks.

"That's what it looks like. And she's homeless in more ways than one. Even her first home, the old Wooden House at the bottom of the Lake is coming apart under the weight of the water. Its wooden beams come off and slowly float upward, first the roof, then the walls, the wooden chairs, the floor, until nothing is left of the Wooden House at the bottom of the Lake. And the Woman feels the pangs of a deep loss, but she doesn't know what caused it, because in a way she's happy to not be with the Dandy any more. She walks the seedy streets of the City, mingling with prostitutes and johns."

"What are those?" Tyler asks.

"It's like when you have a business you sell a product and the clients buy it, right? Well, prostitutes are women who sell their bodies and johns are what you call their clients."

"But how does a woman—"

"That's all you need to know at this point, so that you understand the goddamn story. But lemme just add here that that's not the kinda business any woman wants to be in. Well, come to think of it there *was* this one woman in Tijuana… but anyway, beside the point. Point is, it's a bad business to be in, not least 'cause the bosses in this line of work are very cruel. A woman boss is called a Madam, and there she is standing by a doorway, puffing on a cigarette, sizing up our Woman, sensing her weakness. The Madam motions to the Woman to follow her inside. The Woman, still shivering, still hungry, ponders for a moment but finally she enters the brothel. Her new workplace."

"Can we skip this part, Dad?"

"No, son, it wouldn't be fair to the story, now would it? But I'll give you a clean version of it," Landon says. "Imagine the Woman lying under the sheets on her side of the bed, so you can't see if she's naked or not, and then imagine a series of johns, all dressed in their street clothes, occupying the other side of the bed, one after another. As one john goes, another comes, pardon the pun, and on and on. The Woman barely moves in these images, the only discernible difference in the Woman is her make-up, hairdo, and *age*. Somewhere in the middle of that sequence we spot our Man. He's just another john, he and the Woman are now strangers to one another, come together again for only a brief moment before leaving as strangers. And the Hands of Time keep moving. Tick-tock, tick-tock, tick-tock…"

"What about the Man's johns, did he have any of his own?"

"The Man had lovers. Now picture the scene before, only the Man lies dressed in his Sunday best in his own bed, his lovers next to him."

"What are his lovers wearing?" Tyler asks.

"Well, I dreamed them naked, truth be told, and that's the way I prefer to remember them, if you don't mind, but you go ahead and put some clothes on 'em. And just like the Woman before, our Man also goes through a series of transformations, like his hairline receding, his mustache growing, his wrinkles getting more pronounced. In other words, he's aging quite a bit himself. And why is that?"

"The Hands of Time?"

"Bingo! Time spares no one, and the Woman is now an *old* Woman," Landon says. "She is a bit hunched over and walks with the use of a cane. She passes by the Clock Tower but doesn't even look over. She has no recollection whatsoever of where she's come from or what she's supposed to be doing there. It's been so long the waters have already subsided, and what was once a lake is now a valley again. Do you remember what was at the bottom of that Green Valley?"

"Her house! Their Wooden House," Tyler blurts out.

"The house is no more, it got destroyed in the flood. But there's something else, buried there in the dirt," Landon says.

"The Snow Globe! The twin Snow Globe with the tiny house inside!"

"This is no ordinary Snow Globe. It shoots up a sprout like it's some kinda plant, a living thing. The sprout pierces the surface of the earth. The seed has taken," Landon says.

The Times are changing and the Woman, as fate has it, passing by a novelty store she spots a Snow Globe in the window. On impulse, as if guided by a mysterious hand, she walks into the store. The Woman holds the

Snow Globe in her hands. It's not just any other Snow Globe, it's the very Snow Globe she had lost ages ago. Sure enough, there's a little Wooden House inside the globe. She smiles with sudden recognition and says, "I know that House". The Woman counts the little change she has in her pocket and pays for it. The Snow Globe has now returned to its rightful owner, and she couldn't be more pleased about it. The Woman cradles her Snow Globe under her arm like a newborn. She's heading somewhere only she knows, and her mind is now more determined than ever. She nearly runs through the cobblestone streets, brushing by a passerby, almost knocking him over. This passerby is our Man, now an old Man. He turns slightly to get a closer look at the old Woman holding her Snow Globe like a baby and a sparkle of recognition flashes on his face. "I know that Woman," the Man says to no one but himself, and starts following her. "I know that Woman from somewhere," he repeats. The Woman sees a patch of green in the distance, past the stone monoliths of the cityscape. She heads that way. The Man follows her, keeping his distance. The Woman walks along a path through the forest, the same one she had walked in the beginning, only in the opposite direction. She walks like she had walked that road countless times before and, before long, she finds herself at a spot overlooking a glorious valley. The Green Valley. She stops for a moment to catch her breath as she takes in the beauty of the valley she knows so well. She cuddles the Snow Globe and smiles as she realizes what had happened.

"What happened?" asks Tyler.

"Over the sound of the Clock Tower ticking away, picture that," Landon says, "we see the buried Snow Globe spring more sprouts, growing out of the small Wooden House in the middle, which acts like a seed. There's a wall funneling slowly out of the ground, along with a chimney. The tiny front porch spirals into a tube pointing upward. The tube worms its way towards the surface like a root. Before you know it, the entire Wooden House has sprung up from that seed in the Snow Globe and rests now, just like before but renewed and fresh, in the center of that beautiful Green Valley."

"Whoa," Tyler says.

The sight of the Wooden House overwhelms the Man as well, and he stands there frozen as old memories flood back in. He walks toward the house, opens the door and sees the Woman in the far corner. She smiles in recognition. The Man approaches her. He grabs her wrinkly, age-worn hands and kisses them. "My love, you have grown old," he says.

The Woman turns her head slightly toward a mirror that hangs on a wall. The Man spots his own reflection in the mirror and gasps. To their amazement, their youth has been restored. They touch their own faces, their hands, in complete disbelief. The Woman runs her hand over her belly.

She's pregnant.

Traffic has let up somewhat and Landon weaves through the lanes, trying to make up for the wasted time. All the while he's bringing his story to an end. "Holding hands, the Man and the Woman step outside the house. Light comes in through the open door, reflecting off the Snow Globe on the table, the one the Woman had brought back from the City. Inside the Snow Globe there's a tiny Wooden House, with a miniature couple standing in front of it, holding hands. A dark shade passes over it, and I awake."

"The end," Tyler says.

"The end, but there's a kicker to the story."

"What do you mean?"

"There's something I held back from you," Landon says. "You see, the Man in the dream is me, and the Woman in the dream is your mother."

"But didn't you say you had the dream *before* you met Mom?" Tyler asks.

"Yeah, and when I saw her in real life, I recognized her as the woman in my dream. That's how I knew she was the one for me."

"And the baby in her belly, is that Jason?"

"I don't know, Tyler. Dreams tell you what you need to know, but they don't tell you all you *want* to know."

"But what does the dream mean?" Tyler asks.

"I'm still trying to figure it out," Landon says. "It might have to do with other lifetimes. Past, future. It's one long journey, son."

"Dad?"

"Yes, Tyler."

"How did you and Mom meet in real life?"

Landon looks up to see the traffic light changing from green to yellow. He powers through the intersection, unaware that Tyler is waiting for an answer that won't come, and the next moments occur to him as if time itself were on a yo-yo, now stretching now contracting, like the hands of time on a berserk clock, and doesn't settle into its natural rhythm until the car stops flipping and skids on its back all the way to a bus stop, leaving a trail of broken glass in its wake, T-boned as it was by Ray Barba's half-sister's second cousin, the Runt.

* * *

Landon kicks the door open and wrestles with the wreckage like a bug trapped in a spider web, landing on his back before getting a handle on which goes up and which goes down. He looks around in a daze, unable to get his bearings until he spots Tyler trapped inside and an urge from the deep unleashes in him the will to save his boy at all costs. It's the kind of single-mindedness that can drive the physical body into feats of unusual strength, defying the laws of nature in a subconscious war of mind over matter, and Landon does not find it strange in the heat of the moment that the hulky metallic mess of the car would move as if on ice at his every push and shove. Still, he tries to yank the back doors open but all he does is manage to break the handles. He calls out his son's name repeatedly, but Tyler is not moving, unconscious or worse.

He spots a gasoline leak pooling fast underneath the car and realizes he only has seconds before the car explodes. His next thought is that he would die with his son, right there in those banal surroundings, a dreary bus stop, as uninspiring and profane a setting he can think of. Strangely, that brings about calmness over him, a comfort in knowing that he would never abandon his son, not even in the afterlife, and he experiences a freedom he has never felt before.

His actions turn machine-like as he kicks the trunk open and grabs a crowbar. He smashes the rear window with mechanical precision, his already damaged hand sending shivers of pain through his body. He crawls inside the back of the car and unfastens Tyler's safety belt.

"Tyler, Tyler!" he cries, not stopping for a moment, but Tyler does not respond. Landon kicks into the rear door, his breathing laborious, looking like he's about to faint at any moment. Yet he keeps at it with the will of an automatic shotgun. At last the door gives in and it flings open. Landon uses his last drop of energy to drag Tyler out of the wreckage and carry him to safety.

* * *

Landon spots Ray standing in the middle of the road, hobbling around and yelling into his cell phone. A flash of rage strikes Landon, a sentiment outdone only by his need to hold his son in his arms at all costs, and then by the ball of real fire that bursts from his exploding car like a solar flare, knocking him down to the ground and sucking the oxygen out of his lungs.

The Traveler stands watching from across the street, and Landon catches a glimpse of him through the billowing smoke. "You see, you see," Landon appears to tell the Traveler, though his lips aren't moving, "I would never abandon my son. How do you like that? I'm no coward. What happened with Jason is another story. You don't understand. I wasn't *there* with him when he died but he was with me and I was with him, body and soul. You oughta know. *Body and soul*, motherfucker. Don't be so quick to judge me. I would never abandon my boys. You wanna know what happened that night, don't you? I'll tell you what happened…" But just like that the smoke drifts away and so does the Traveler, and Landon finds himself mumbling to himself, as the sound of sirens amplifies with each passing moment.

* * *

An hour later Landon finally comes to in a hospital ward, bruised and burned on one side, a big bandage on his hand. He wastes no time fending off an army of nurses to locate his son in the Intensive Care Unit. He approaches the bed where Tyler lies unconscious, though clinically still alive, hooked up to IV bags and monitoring devices that make him look like a spider, much like the girl Landon prayed for in another hospital a few days prior.

Landon plants a kiss on his son's forehead. "Hey, Tyler. Daddy's here." Melanie and Dr. Miller stand bedside but in that moment they are as real to Landon as ghosts. The doctor tells him the next forty-eight hours are critical, the boy's life hanging in balance, and Landon feels so impotent he wishes he could consult an oracle. A million different thoughts are racing through his mind and one of those might save him. Melanie, ever the practical woman, demands answers by her mere presence, and Landon is at a loss to explain what has happened or even come up with a credible scenario. He hears her ask something about insurance. He can't tell for sure who was at fault, he's already blanked out the last minute leading up to the impact. He can't recall for sure making the last car insurance payment either. He feels the weight of the world as he summons up the higher powers. Melanie tells the doctor that the boy's not covered but please don't treat him any different, she'll pay somehow. Landon says, "I'll see what I can scrape up," and that brings a sarcastic laugh out of Melanie but to her surprise he pulls out a check and asks for a pen. She finds one on a doctor's clipboard and

Landon signs the check over to her. "What's this?" she asks, staring incredulously at the large dollar figure.

"My father's house. I just sold it."

"But Landon—"

"I don't wanna hear it."

"Don't think you're off the hook now," Melanie says. "I'm gonna need to fill out some paperwork, and when I come back I better not hear some bullshit story."

* * *

Landon takes note of a second bed in the hospital room and wonders why it's taken him so long to notice it. It's as if it just appeared there out of thin air. There are white drapes surrounding it, which billow slightly in the air-conditioned draft, and there appear to be someone resting in the bed, his contour barely visible through the gossamer sheets. This patient is reposed and still as a mummy.

"Hello," Landon says, testing the waters, but the patient is silent.

Now assured of his privacy, Landon turns his full attention to his son and addresses him in a low voice, as if to confess something of a deeply personal and secret nature. "You gonna be all right, Tyler, you hear me. When I was a kid, my own daddy had a run-in with some pretty bad people. I don't know if I ever told you about this. It was over a racehorse, a mare named Bardo Hollywood, my dad raised her like a child, swear to God she ate better'n me on most days. She won some races early on and some scary people decided to invest in the horse, like it was a sure bet. Wasn't my dad's idea, they just left him no choice. So when the mare got hurt one day those scary folks asked for their money back plus interest and my dad said, well, I ain't got the money, I put all that money in training the horse, so fuck off. And that's how my dad got the living shit beat out of him and ended up in a coma. And the bad guys took a saw to the poor mare and, I heard, made salami out of the poor animal, as was the custom in their home country. Lemme tell you though, I have tasted the best dry salami once, it was a deli up in the valley on, I wanna say Devonshire... they cut the salami up in square slices and I was told it was made outta horse meat. Not saying that Bardo Hollywood made for good salami, for chrissakes, can't even think about it, I loved that horse, just saying this was one lean horse, prime muscle everywhere, and those shoulder chucks, man... but... Anyway, back to the story, my dad, your granddad, got hit in the head real hard and was in a coma for a week. Everyone thought he was gonna die, even the doctors said to unplug him. But not me, because, you see, I'd made a deal with... Management. Get it? I said to Them, or to Him, or Her, god knows, I said, take a year out of my life and give it to Dad. The higher-ups said, after some debate, not a problem. How did I know, you ask? I just did, I felt it inside, and it felt like a definite yes. Thing is, you gotta be serious about it, dead serious 'cause there's no going back. You put that wish out there and it's gone with the wind, baby. You wanna return that for a refund, you're shit outta luck, that boat has sailed, you gotta live with the consequences. Why just one year? I don't know, it was a tryout, wanted to see if it works. Honest, I didn't even know you could cut out a deal like that. No, wait, I did read something along those lines, some ancient hero, can't remember his name, asked his witch wife Medea to take a few years off his life and give 'em to his dying father. Or was it *you* told me that story, something you read in your books? Anyhow, don't know if the witchcraft worked, but those two lovebirds didn't end up too good in the end. That Medea, a witch spurned— you don't wanna know. But, hey, I'm pretty sure it worked with me. Shit, had I known earlier I woulda done it more often," Landon laughs, "with my luck, I probably woulda been dead by now. I'm tellin' you, Tyler, had my dad died that day he woulda been a hero in my book. Forever. Certified hero. Funny how things work out. But you get what I'm saying, yeah? A deal's a deal. It feels again like a definite yes to me, so there… You can thank me later and, pray to Management, you won't grow up to hate me. Oh, and another thing, if you're hearing this, and I'm sure you are on some level, this stays between us. Over and out, son."

The door opens and, to Landon's disbelief, in walks Ray, sporting a neck brace and walking with the help of a cane. "Breaks my heart to see him like this. He's a good kid, got caught in the crossfire." Ray says. "But shit happens, then *more* shit happens."

"You got some balls walking in here like this. You know you can get even more hospitalized than you already are," Landon says.

Ray saunters to the window, the walking cane sounding the cadence. "I was worried about you for a minute."

"Yeah?"

"When you didn't show up last night I thought something might've happened to you," Ray says. "It's a dangerous world out there when you're sitting on a million-dollar bounty."

"You don't say," Landon says, his good hand still caressing his son's body.

"But I see you're doing just fine. I mean, under the circumstances."

"Is that a good thing or a bad thing?"

"Well, that depends, doesn't it," Ray says. "When you're hurt you're prone to get better. When you're fine you stand to get hurt. And so it goes."

"So it goes," Landon agrees.

"Listen, I know why you're doing this. But you're wrong about one thing. I do love Melanie, and I believe the sentiment is mutual. This is my family now. I can be a good parent to your boy if you'll only let me," Ray says.

"I don't trust you," Landon says. "I'm a small-time crook, I admit it, but I know one when I see one and you're nothing but a thug. Yeah, just like me, a goddamn *thuggee*."

"For your own good, I'm still hoping you do the right thing and return the stolen goods to *me*, the rightful owner," Ray says. "At some point you'll have to think what a truck full of cigarettes would be worth in human terms. What could I possibly take from you to make up for that loss?"

"You're trying to take my family away from me. That's gotta count for something," Landon says.

"The family that you abandoned and betrayed years ago? I'm not the one who got you divorced and I'm not the one skipping on child support payments," Ray says, and points his walking cane at Landon like he's about to shoot him. "It's time you let go so they get on with their lives. They don't need you as much as you think."

Landon squeezes Tyler's hand and addresses him like he was standing there fully conscious. "Don't listen to this idiot. I'll never give up on you, Tyler."

"I can hurt you, Landon. I told you once that I can find you no matter where you're hiding," Ray says.

"And—"

"You're here, ain't you?"

"All evidence points to it," Landon says.

Ray turns to leave. He makes a few steps toward the door then stops briefly before dropping a farewell salvo. "I wish Tyler a speedy recovery. I hope he doesn't share his brother's fate, dying alone while his father's in the company of whores." If Ray's intention is to provoke then it's mission accomplished, because Landon leaps out like a ninja and is on Ray's back before the last syllable of "You slimy motherfucker!" rolls off his tongue with gusto.

The two men drop on the floor and quickly land a few awkward punches that miss their target. They are at each other's throats like that and, as blood drains out of their faces, it looks like they're gonna simultaneously choke each other to death and a moment before it's too late a roar blasts through the room, loud enough to bring the hostilities to a sudden halt.

Both Landon and Ray glance over at the mystery patient, the only possible source for the lionesque ten-hut call, but the sheets around his bed are barely rippling and all is dead quiet again.

Barring no further explanation for the intrusion, their eyes slowly turn back to each other and the truce is over. Landon gets Ray in a headlock and proceeds to drag him in a circle around the room like in a wrestling contest as security and a couple of intrepid nurses barge into the room. But no one can make Landon loosen his grip.

Through the window facing the hallway Melanie peers into the ICU room to see a pile of human bodies wrestling in slow motion on the floor: security personnel, nurses, Ray, Landon. It looks like an orgy gone terribly wrong.

Landon screams from deep under, "Fuckin' murderer! Keep your hands off my kid... Or I'm gonna shit on your face."

Accusations fly back and forth like a truth-or-dare laser show and it doesn't take long for Melanie to figure out what has brought everyone together this sunny day.

As two security guards drag Landon out of the room he hears the metallic clink of Melanie's engagement ring bounce off the floor, and Ray saying, "Are you out of your mind?" then Melanie replying "No, you're out of *my* fucking mind, asshole!"

Landon prods her on, "You tell him, Mel!" appealing to her good side but the door shuts behind him.

When Landon gets kicked out the back door of the hospital he's actually grateful the rent-a-cops didn't call in the real cops, else he'd need to deal with a restraining order that might force him away from Tyler. But he can't keep Melanie at bay. He barely has time to straighten himself up when Melanie is in his face with the big question. "Did you have anything to do with that stolen truck, Landon?" she asks, her eyes locked just inches away from his. Landon stutters, starts to say something but changes his mind, and when he sees Melanie relax her body and snap her head back he knows that she already knows, and he stops making any effort at dancing around the answer.

Melanie makes a paper ball out of the check he's given her and tosses it at his feet before walking back inside.

"Can I call you later? Talk about this—" Landon says, but she's already gone, and he knows there'd be weeks, if not months, before she looks at him like a human being again.

The whole scene leaves Landon with a bitter taste in his mouth, as if all the vanities in the Book of Ecclesiastes have taken physical form and a potion made of those ingredients have been forced down his throat like medicine by a cruel doctor.

*"You will recognize them
   like the meeting
between mother and son
   or
like seeing old friends again."*

The Tibetan Book of the Dead, Day Six

Seated at a table at Norm's, Landon can't help but notice a slight change in the dynamics of their three-strong wrecking crew. Stephanie, who'd usually sit next to him and rub against his thigh like a tabby cat, is now seated across the table and next to Frankie. It signals to Landon a shift of allegiances that he's not quite ready to deal with right now, but he carries on just the same. "He's a fucking animal, that guy, he won't think twice before hurting my kid again," Landon says. "Do you understand? My kid's in a coma, and anything happens to him... I can't have that on my conscience. So, I've thought it over and I've decided not to call the Chinaman. Yeah, I'm giving Ray his fucking truck back." He takes a sip of his coffee, awaiting judgment, which like a Chinese drop is slow in coming.

Stephanie and Frankie shift in their seats and trade knowing glances before she steps up to the mic. "Actually, we beg to differ," she says. She looks at Frankie for moral support, but his mind appears to be entirely engrossed by the tuna sandwich in front of him.

"I've already made up my mind, and guess what, it's over," Landon says.

"Well, fuck you, man," Stephanie explodes, making a few heads in the busy diner turn, before bringing the volume down a notch, "I want my fuckin' share. We made a deal. I helped you steal the damn truck. Now I want what's mine."

"A bit inconsiderate, huh, given what I'm going through," Landon says, waiting for Frankie to cast the deciding vote. "Some sympathy here?"

"She's got a point," Frankie says, inadvertently spitting out a chunk of tuna in Landon's direction.

"You in this together?" Landon says. "You talked it over and came here with a plan, didn't you?" And this one's meant for Frankie, "Unified front, right, union boss?"

"Yo, man, it's capitalism, y'know, and she's got a point. Besides, I really feel like putting the hurt on that Ray dude," Frankie says. "With him outta the picture, your kid's safe, we keep the loot, everybody's happy. Think about it."

"I don't know about that," Landon says. "Guy's like a cornered animal, he's connected and he's dangerous."

"I want my goddamn share, okay?" Stephanie says. "You wanna just sell enough to pay me and Frankie here, we can roll with that, too."

"I suppose you found a buyer…" Landon says.

"The Chinaman," Frankie says.

"I'm not calling the Chinaman," Landon says. "You hear me?"

"Five by five, bro, don't worry about it," Frankie says "'Cause I already have. We're going to Chinatown tonight. He's expecting us."

"How'd you do that? You don't even know the guy, you're pig fodder to him, you're gonna get yourselves killed," Landon says.

"That's why you'll be tagging along," Frankie says.

"And why would I do that?"

"'Cause when I called I said I was *you*," Frankie mumbles. "Goddamn gook couldn't tell the difference." Landon jolts out of his seat, rushes outside and stops at the entrance, his heart beating so fast he thinks it's a panic attack if not a full-on cardiac arrest. He closes his eyes to calm himself down and when he opens them again he finds himself face to face with a toothless bum begging for alms, a vision which startles him out of his skin and back into the diner, five bucks lighter.

"C'mon, that's what friends do," Frankie says. "All the shit we been through, bro, you gonna let me down now?" Stephanie reaches across the table and squeezes Landon's hands in her first show of affection in days.

"Dem fools ain't seen nothin' yet!" Frankie says and gently parts his camo jacket to reveal a brand-new Springfield Armory 1911. "War is coming," he says, and twitches like someone just shoved a cattle prod up his ass. "Goddamn, man, I threw my back again!" Frankie says.

"You just need another massage, Frankie," Stephanie says.

"*Another*?" Landon says. "Massages don't work on Frankie, don't you know?"

"Why wouldn't they work on him? They work on everybody." she says.

"Because of Ozone," Landon says.

"Ozone?! What the fuck does that have to do with the price of tea in China?" Stephanie asks, and Landon proceeds to tell her the story of Ozone, the brave bullet catcher who saved Frankie's life back in Iraq, which is how Ozone got his nickname in the first place. Landon was driving an armor-kit free Humvee near the front of a convoy that fateful day, Frankie riding shotgun while lost in deep thoughts about a blonde Cali beach girl named Jezebel and backseat blowjobs on the Fourth of July when an IED popped under the Stryker in front of them, instantly killing its occupants. A piece of IED shrapnel flew clean through Landon's shoulder, which made him yank the steering wheel, a maneuver that, coupled with the explosion blast, caused the vehicle to flip over and land on its side, sending Frankie flying like a trapeze artist and landing unconscious, no surprise there, in the middle of the road while the rest of the convoy pulled to the side to take shelter from the incoming guerilla fire. That left Frankie lying there like roadkill as the sole exposed piece of meat Made in U.S.A., and it was only due to the insurgents' bad aim or shaky hands or just sheer dumb luck on Frankie's part that the first bullet hail took bites out of the asphalt instead. While everyone was looking to counter the attack and made frantic calls for air backup it was the nineteen-year-old kid Ozone Layer who had the presence of mind to jump into the middle of the road, roll his body on top of Frankie's, and in one smooth move hoist Frankie onto his back and swiftly carry him to safety. A rain of bullets fell upon them like so many personal insults but miraculously only one hit the target, this while Ozone was directly on top of Frankie, piercing first Ozone's hip before making its way to Frankie's right butt cheek, where it nestled for a few hours until surgery. Ozone then, for good measure, climbed into the upturned Humvee and dragged Landon out to safety. How Ozone was able to accomplish that feat with a broken hip is anyone's guess, but the fact remains that some sort of miracle occurred that day and Landon firmly believes that all of Frankie's subsequent health complications stemmed from his lack of gratefulness in the face of such divine intervention by means of a human shield, perfect but for the one bullet hole. Hence, Ozone Layer.

Ozone Layer, it turned out, had to face his own demons down the road and eventually took his own life by way of bullet to the head in the bathtub with the kids asleep upstairs. What made Ozone kill himself Landon never found out, but he couldn't help wishing that he didn't have to suffer much in the afterlife, what with suicide being much frowned upon in all traditions, and secretly suspected that whatever people called Hell, or at least a version of it, was actually right down here on Earth, no two ways about it. Landon mourned him like he was family but the news of Ozone offing himself came as a relief to Frankie, who for the previous couple of years going back to the incident had to play the unwilling role of army buddy to someone he saw as a dumb hick to whom he wouldn't otherwise extend anything past the courtesy of a salute if not for the fact that the rube had saved his life and the two were thus forever tied into a karmic knot. Ozone felt within his rights to call Frankie at all hours of the day and night and when calls went unanswered he'd show up at Frankie's door carrying a backpack and a case of booze. He would crash on Frankie's couch for a couple days, shooting the shit and bitching about his life on a farm in Mystic, Georgia, and then he'd vanish just as quickly as he'd appeared, giving no signs of life for weeks at a time. To say that Frankie hated him is to state the obvious. "What is this, feudal Japan? Guy saves my life, now I'm his indentured servant? Way of the fuckin' samurai?" Frankie complained one day upon returning to LA from Mystic, Georgia, where he had just spent a week with Ozone and his newly wedded wife, Sherry Lee. "This is bullshit, man. I want my life back. Jeezuz."

Long story short, nothing a massage would fix.

* * *

They spend most of the day arguing over how many cigarette cartons they should bring to the trading table to whet the feared mobster's appetite without insulting him, and the agreed upon limit is whatever they could fit inside Stephanie's Mustang, including the glove box. The idea being that if the overture goes down as planned they'd sell half the loot the next day and allow Landon to return the truck to Ray. It'd be missing half its cargo, sure, but Landon takes the glass half-full approach to the problem and is certain that he could come up with some excuse or other and cut a deal with Ray where he'd stay alive and his son safe even if it meant relocating to a foreign land or becoming Ray's personal chauffeur and door mat. Anyway, he'd cross that bridge when he gets to it.

Landon could use a second opinion and it doesn't help that Cassidy's oracle kid isn't at the truck shop to settle the matter by way of peeking through the cosmic veil. Turns out, the boy is grounded on account of, Cassidy says, *sticky fingers*. And he gesticulates it to make his point. He explains how Val has developed a crush on his school-teacher and his curious nature drove him to pilfer any little thing out of her purse, for later study at home, until he inevitably was caught red handed sniffing one of her, thankfully sealed, tampons and got promptly expelled. Cassidy wasted no time in applying the requisite corrections to his son's behavior, meaning leather to bare ass on repeat, and when later in the day he wondered how long he'd need to ground that punk to teach him a lesson he dragged him out of the dark closet to find the answer through divination. It was seven days. Grounded, no TV, no stealing, no sniffing, no divination. Seven days longer than Landon could afford.

* * *

They reach Chinatown after nightfall and Landon finds himself in the back seat of the car, rather than in the front next to Stephanie, staring absentmindedly at the bright neon signs, the colors blurring in his peripheral vision as if the buildings themselves dissolved into light and this perception spawns in Landon the idea that everything is light, everything we see and everything we don't see, even time itself, just light taking the form of matter, at the same time infinite and yet subject to some divine being, perhaps awakening from a deep divine lumber replete with ferocious nightmares, making this whole rigmarole disappear with the flick of a cosmic switch, just like that. Wouldn't that be something, to go out like a light. Is there anything better he could hope for at this moment in time? He doubts it.

"Where the hell is this place?" Stephanie asks, but Landon doesn't seem to hear her, he only sees a flickering dark spectrum with jello arms occupying roughly the driver's seat.

"Landon, we lost or what?" Frankie nudges him.

Landon snaps out of the trance and quickly orients himself. "Turn right over there, where is says Moon Cycle Shiatsu. Into the alleyway."

* * *

The car pulls up in the rear parking lot of the Red Pagoda Restaurant, which boasts precisely two spots *for customer only*, one of which is vacant. A lone fluorescent light casts a milkish hue over the area. A restaurant worker hurls a couple of heavy-duty trash bags into a nearby dumpster then licks his fingers.

"I think we'll wait for you in the car, bro," Frankie says.

"What the hell are you talking about? You made the call, you set this up. It wasn't my choice. I'll need some backup in there," Landon says.

"As I recall, it's money *you* owe us," Frankie says, then turns to Stephanie, "Am I right? I made the call, least you can do is go in there and sell some fucking cigarettes."

"I'm scared, I need someone to stay here with me," Stephanie says. To make her point she keeps the engine running, radio still on.

"You shoulda stayed home in the first place," Landon says.

"Yeah, right, and let you get away with all that money. Screw you, Landon," she says.

"I'm not going in there by myself," Landon says to Stephanie, "This is the dude, rumor has it, that cut another dude in half, with an ax, over a gambling debt. Like, in the parking lot he did that. Ask Frankie here, he'll tell you all about it."

"That's just a rumor, bro, I wouldn't take it seriously," Frankie says, as payback.

"We're probably sitting in the very spot. And besides—"

"Are you gonna chicken out now?" Stephanie asks.

"Besides," Landon says, "it's just a thing with these guys, they won't like it one bit if we don't all go in. Shows lack of respect. Or something."

"They don't even know we're here," Stephanie says, just as a burly bouncer comes around the side of the car and checks it out briefly with a flashlight before waddling back inside.

"Now they do," Landon says.

"What, you know that guy? He work here?" Frankie asks.

"Yeah, I've seen him around once or twice," Landon says.

"What's his name?"

"I don't fuckin' know," Landon says. "They go by nicknames. Lil Panda, or something."

Stephanie rolls her eyes, "That's such a cliché."

"Hey, I didn't name the motherfucker," Landon says, "*They* did. And don't get fooled, there's nothing cute about him."

"You afraid you gonna end up in Lil Panda's California roll?" Frankie says, flapping his arms around like chicken wings.

"They're Chinese, Frankie," Landon says.

"Why they call 'em *California* rolls, then, huh? Tell me that," Frankie says, and Stephanie has a good laugh, which made her relax a little.

"Would you turn off the engine?" Landon says to her. "Please." Frankie nods a subtle 'no' in her direction, but she pretends not to see it and kills the engine.

"Listen, business to them is personal, y'know," Landon says, "They gotta get to know you. It's no big deal, trust me, all you need to do is sit down for a cup of tea or a soup or something, smell some fuckin' incense, and we'll be outta there in no time. Really, how hard can that be? The longer we wait here the more suspicious they'll get." Stephanie sighs, and Frankie puts a consoling hand on her thigh, which Landon files in his mind as something to talk about at a later time.

"What the fuck, we only got so much merch on us anyway," Frankie says. "They stiff us, we go right back to the well. More where that came from."

"He's gonna try to lowball us, so we gotta stand firm," Landon says. "Once we agree on a price then we bring in the rest of it. Agreed?"

"All right, but let's make it quick. I give you the cigarettes, you gimme the money. See ya later," Stephanie says.

"And let me do the talking," Landon says.

"Wait a minute. You gonna drag me in there but expect me to shut my mouth. That's not how I roll, bro,"

Frankie says. "Something on my mind I'mna go ahead say it."

"Yeah, well, that's why American businesses don't do well in China. If you care to know. Cause they don't get this human touch aspect of it," Landon says.

"It's true," Stephanie chimes in, "In Shanghai, I was there a few years ago, I went to this huge Barbie store, five stories high, just beautiful. American as apple pie, but last I heard they shut it down."

"See?" Landon says, still wondering how come she'd never brought that up in conversation, even after hammering her daily with his infatuation with that culture.

"Ok, just pop the trunk already. Let's load up," Frankie says, and the team gets to work. "I mean, I know they tried," Stephanie continues, "hell, they even made a Chinese Barbie. Her name was Ling."

"Well," Landon says, as he hurls a bag over his shoulder, "I guess the writing was on the wall soon as they came out with Ling's male companion— *Ding-a-Ling*."

* * *

Lil Panda holds the back door open as the three amigos haul large burlap bags chock-full of cigarettes inside the establishment, then guides them down some barely lit labyrinthine hallways to a room covered almost completely in velvety red-and-gold srivatsas.

Mr. Zhang, an elderly man dressed up in a blue suit, sits on a high royal velvet chair. His eyes are closed yet he appears to possess an awareness that goes beyond the senses. He nods gently and his henchmen dump the contents of the bags at Mr. Zhang's feet like war spoils.

"Made in America, boys," Landon grins, alone in a room of stone faces. Mr. Zhang motions at a henchman, who promptly picks out a carton at random and opens it. He takes a cigarette out of a pack and hands it to his boss. Mr. Zhang holds the cigarette about an inch away from his mouth until one of his men scrambles to light it up.

Mr. Zhang takes a deep puff out of the cigarette and finally opens his eyes. He has Landon square in his eyesight when he suddenly throws a coughing fit so violent he drops the cigarette on the floor.

"Not your brand, huh?" Landon says.

The henchman scrambles to light up another cigarette for his boss. Mr. Zhang takes another hit and predictably goes coughing like a donkey again, this time even louder and longer.

"Are you all right?" Landon asks after some time.

"No, I'm sick man. Very ill," Mr. Zhang says, and nods gravely like a man who's chosen the wrong path and is now seen as the negative example to be followed only at one's own peril.

"Sorry to hear it," Landon says.

"Cancer of the throat," Mr. Zhang says.

Feeling left out somehow, Frankie jumps in, "From smoking?" Mr. Zhang laughs, says something in Chinese and mimics licking a pussy, using for demonstration purpose the common pictograph of the triangle made of joining the opposing index fingers and thumbs, respectively. His whole crew erupts with laughter. Frankie gives him the thumbs up, like he's in on the joke but no one pays any attention to him.

"We have a saying, a cigarette after dinner is better than life after death," Mr. Zhang says. He barks out some orders and a beautiful young Chinese girl enters the room, dressed up in a silk robe, her high eyebrow arches and pale make-up producing the impression of a moving porcelain figurine. She takes her place next to Mr. Zhang, picks up a hand-rolled cigarette off a silver tray, lights it up, takes a puff and gently blows the smoke in his face, making it look like his head is hanging in a low cloud in the sky. Landon thinks it's the sexiest thing he's ever seen. The girl blowing smoke, that is.

"You have more," Mr. Zhang says to Landon.

"Say again?" Landon says, still in awe of the smoking girl.

"You have more, I know you wouldn't bother me over this much cigarettes, so let's talk real business, yes?"

"There's more where that came from, yes. But this is all I'm selling tonight," Landon says. "Let's work this out and settle on a price, then I bring in more tomorrow. That work for you?"

"I buy everything, all of it, tonight. Or no deal."

"It's not all mine to give, y'know," Landon says, looking at Frankie and Stephanie to back him up, which they do with slight nods of approval. "Think of me as a middleman."

"You worried about price," Mr. Zhang says.

"We haven't discussed a price," Landon says, glancing at his crew.

"Yes, yes, price is negotiable," Mr. Zhang says.

"I mean for the whole lot," Landon says. "I—*we* haven't figured out a price yet. I suggest we negotiate a price for this, what's on the floor here, now."

"You need cash tonight," Mr. Zhang says.

"For this load, yeah. I prefer everything up front," Landon says, his voice slightly trembling all of a sudden.

"So do I. Everything on the up and up." Mr. Zhang yells out some instructions in Chinese, then throws his head back to take in another cloud of cigarette smoke. "Cash is on the way," Mr. Zhang says. "I have many laundromats in five block area. May take some time to collect, so make your selves comfortable. I hope you take payment in quarter dollar coins." There is an awkward silence for a few seconds, Landon and Frankie exchanging glances, then Mr. Zhang bursts out laughing. "Only joking. I like to joke."

A waitress comes in with a tray of exquisite China teacups and Mr. Zhang says something to her and she serves his guests first, after making sure they are all properly seated at a table in front of the boss. Mr. Zhang points at Landon and Frankie. "You two, brothers?" Mr. Zhang asks.

"Blood brothers, man," Frankie says.

"How do you mean?"

Frankie rolls his eyes and Landon feels the need to jump in to avoid any contentious follow-up. "The blood spilled in battle is thicker than the water of the womb," Landon says, "is what we mean by that."

"Interesting notion," Mr. Zhang says.

Frankie takes his flask out of his jacket and pours some whiskey into his cup of tea. He then tastes the brew and keeps nodding. "How about you fellas? You brothers, too? I mean, you ask me, you kinda look alike. Not necessarily on account of the eyes or skin pigment, I ain't one of those guys—"

"We are karma brothers," Mr. Zhang interrupts.

"How does that work?" Frankie asks.

"We have predestined relationships. Karma runs thicker than blood—spilled, shared, shaken or stirred."

"Hey, I know what you mean by that," Landon says, and gets up to take a closer look at the room. "Having crossed paths I guess that makes us karma cousins or something."

Frankie upturns his whiskey flask and gives it a few taps in the behind until the last drop of the liquor slides mercifully into his teacup. "I'll drink to that, cuz," he says to Mr. Zhang.

Landon spots a horse trinket on top of a shelf. It looks just like the one Mr. Briggs Sr. had given him for Tyler but ended up in a trashcan on Fairfax well before its expiration date. Landon picks it up to take a closer look. "I've seen one of these before. Tibetan, right?" he asks.

"It's Tibetan windhorse, yes," Mr. Zhang says.

"I'd like to think I know my horses, but I've never heard of that. What the hell's a *wind* horse?" Landon asks.

"Tibetans say it's like the soul," Mr. Zhang says, while inhaling another puff of second-hand smoke.

"In what way?" Landon asks.

"If you don't know, I can't tell you," Mr. Zhang says. "But it's how it got its name."

"What do they call it, like in their own language?" Landon says.

"They call it *Lungta*," Mr. Zhang says.

"Say again?" Landon asks.

"Lung-dah."

"That in Tibetan?"

"I believe so," Mr. Zhang says.

"What's his name in American?" Landon asks.

"You want to know its name in American?" Mr. Zhang laughs, "It's your language, Landon. Call him what you want."

"I'll call it Landon. Close enough," Landon says.

"Fair enough, yes. Landon, *American Soul Horse*," Mr. Zhang says, mocking the idea. "You put that on gravestone."

A henchman arrives like a minister from a troubled foreign land and takes a bow in front of Mr. Zhang. He holds in his hand a briefcase, which he opens at his boss's command. Mr. Zhang takes out a few bricks of cash and tosses them in Landon's direction.

Landon rifles through the wads of cash and nods.

"Yes, yes?" Mr. Zhang says.

"Looking good," Landon says, "Interested in buying more of the same?"

"How much? You tell me how much," Mr. Zhang says. He starts to sound a bit annoyed already, his patience running shorter than a cigarette stub.

"We can bring in four pallets," Landon holds his hand up to about his chin, "yay high. Price per carton, thirty off what you paid today. How's that sound?"

"Half off, or no deal," Mr. Zhang says.

Landon, Frankie and Stephanie get into a quick huddle and decide to go with it. "Deal. And I think I speak for all three of us when I say, it was nice doing business with you, Mr. Zhang," Landon says, already eyeing the exit. The whole thing has gone down better than expected. The notoriously frightening Mr. Zhang appears to be in a good mood, he even laughed a few times, making Landon wonder if the cigarette the Chinaman second-handedly smoked was maybe laced with opium. Hell, maybe he's inhaled some of that opium himself, seeing as he hasn't felt this good since he was in post-deployment recovery, popping Vicodins like Tic Tacs. No matter, it's a glorious feeling, and Landon is ready to celebrate both the deal with the Chinaman and the feeling itself.

* * *

Doesn't last long. The cold shower comes when Landon, having almost made it to the car, feels the hand of god — nay, Lil Panda — yank him back without warning.

"Mr Landon, you come with us," Lil Panda says, and parts his oversized coat to reveal a shiny object, the kind that discourages any further elaboration. Lil Panda then spins around like a public park flasher, making sure they all get the point. Frankie puts his hands up and Stephanie follows suit. "Gimme a call when you can, bro, I'll be standing by," Frankie says, then gets in the car and leaves.

That pretty much settles it for Landon, as far as what to do next. Lil Panda escorts him by the arm into a waiting stretch limousine.

"Where're you taking me?" Landon asks.

Lil Panda opens the door to the limo and shoves Landon inside, where he lands sideways onto the back seat, while the goon keeps watch.

Before long, Mr. Zhang appears, his body framed perfectly by the open door. To Landon's puzzlement,

Mr. Zhang walks into the limo not the normal way, but *backwards*. He trips on his way in, his heel catching the footrest, and the goon is there to offer a hand.

Mr. Zhang aims for the bench closest to the driver. Problem is, Landon has already taken that spot, and for an awkward moment Mr. Zhang's ass hovers in the neighborhood of Landon's face like a cobra ready to pounce. Luckily, Lil Panda comes to the rescue and breaks the standoff by yanking a terrorized Landon over to an adjacent spot. Mr. Zhang sits down with a sigh worth a thousand years.

"What's this all about?" Landon asks.

"Tonight, Mr. Landon, I will teach you about *Death*," Mr. Zhang says.

"Not my favorite subject, death."

"There's more where that came from, yes?" Mr. Zhang says, as he leans in. "You say so yourself."

"You mean death? Yeah, plenty of it to go around, isn't it?"

"No, dummy. Cigarettes. Puff-puff," Mr. Zhang says.

"Oh, cigarettes. Yeah, there's more, but—," Landon trails off, glances out the window and spots the taillights of Stephanie's car vanish around the alleyway. He's alone now.

Mr. Zhang nods with fervor, "Good, good."

"Sorry, we going anywhere?" Landon asks.

"We go to place where more come from," Mr. Zhang says.

"I don't think it's such a good idea," Landon says, "You see, they don't belong to me, they're not mine to give—"

"Tonight I teach you about Death," Mr. Zhang says again. "And there is only one way to learn—the hard way."

Lil Panda rubs his shiny revolver.

"Oh, I see," Landon says. "All right, if that's how it's gonna be."

Landon takes out the keys and business card to Cassidy's Truck Repair Shop and hands them to Mr. Zhang. The Chinaman knocks on the partition window and, as the window rolls down, he hands the directions to the driver. "We go there now," he says, and the limo gets rolling.

"No choice, huh?" Landon says, as his attention is drawn to the techno beats coming in muted forms at first, then louder, from the surrounding speakers, while the changing rainbow colors in the backlit bar make the stretch limo appear like a night club on wheels. Landon recalls the story about Mr. Zhang going psycho at the sight of rainbows, on account of his failed strike on his monk brother and is convinced the Chinaman is using the light show to work himself up into some kind of frenzy, like boxers listening to hip hop or heavy metal to pump themselves up while stepping into an arena before a fight. The lights change colors with the beat of the music, first white, then a soft red, then blue, green, yellow, followed by a soft smoky light that Landon has seen before but only remembers as a strange feeling in his gut.

"But you did have choice, Mr. Landon," Mr. Zhang says, as he puts a hand on Landon's shoulder. Landon feels a shudder shoot down his body all the way through the bottom of his feet.

"Not to worry, I am no longer the man I used to be," Mr. Zhang says, but that doesn't make Landon feel any better, his grasp of reality fading with each passing minute. "The specter of death does that to you," Mr. Zhang says, "Now I think what the Old Me would do, then I do the opposite."

"Is that why you walk backwards?"

"Precisely. Are you familiar with Zhang Guolao?" Mr. Zhang asks.

"Can't say that I am. He work for you?"

"He was one of the Eight Immortals, many centuries ago," Mr. Zhang says.

"Oh. Any relation?"

"Only that he was wise man," Mr. Zhang says, his eyes shut to two narrow slits, "he realized that the world was going backwards, that moral standard it was declining day by day. So, to right the balance, or perhaps just to make a point, he started to ride his donkey backwards."

"Whoa. That's a hell of a donkey," Landon says.

"A donkey's a donkey. A dumb animal," Mr. Zhang says.

"It's hard enough to get a donkey to ride forward, never mind backward. That's what I mean, hell of a donkey," Landon says.

"No, dummy. The donkey... he ride forwards, Zhang Guolao sit on the donkey *facing* backwards." He motions in the direction of the limo. "Limo going forwards, but Mr. Zhang, he be riding backwards, like so," Mr. Zhang says.

"Oh, I see now," Landon says.

"I'm buying you out so you will not find yourself in even more trouble. Which appears to be in your nature," Mr. Zhang says.

"We haven't discussed a price. For the lot, y'know," Landon says.

"No problem, I already set a price." Mr. Zhang points to a briefcase next to Lil Panda. "Down payment. The rest will be delivered as goods are sold."

"I get it, you think you're doing me a favor, instead of sticking it to me like you woulda done back in the day. The New You, it's a miracle, I get it. Paying me in cash on a layaway plan? Well, I don't see it as a favor. I can find a better offer elsewhere," Landon says, but by the looks of it, Mr. Zhang thinks it'd be easier to teach Chinese algebra to a horse. Or a donkey. "With all due respect. Of course," Landon bows ever so slightly to each in turn. "Mr. Zhang, Lil Panda."

"If you say you get it, Landon, then you must realize that it's by virtue of this miracle of the New Me that you and I are still talking." Mr. Zhang motions to

Lil Panda, who places his gun calmly on his lap, pointing at Landon.

"Be cool, man," Landon says.

"You must've heard the rumors of men chopped in half in broad daylight," Mr. Zhang says.

"Oh, yeah."

"That was the Old Me. If someone stole as much as a nickel from me he'd end up in dumpster," Mr. Zhang says. "And a nickel, a nickel is rather impersonal, is it not, it does encourage no feelings of personal attachment or, say, metaphysical musings, if one is so inclined. Never mind an object of spiritual and personal significance to me."

Landon shifts nervously in the hot seat.

"The soul, Landon…"

Mr. Zhang takes in a deep breath and then blows it all out, making a sound like the wind.

Landon gulps, words stuck in his throat.

"I… I don't… know what I was thinking," Landon says, trying to make himself small in an ever-shrinking space capsule. "I'm sorry," he continues, his eyes pleading with the Chinamen, "it's my son, you see, he's in a tight spot—"

Mr. Zhang, eyes closed, keeps blowing. "The soul…" he says.

"My son… he's… he's in a coma," Landon says, "He— That's all I could think about, trying to make him happy."

Mr. Zhang opens his eyes, evaluates Landon at leisure. "The soul, once it leaves your body, finds itself on a journey full of peril. Time is of the essence."

"Yes," Landon says.

"Time is precious."

"I agree with you," Landon says, between sniffling and wiping a few tears. "One hundred percent."

"The soul needs guidance," Mr. Zhang says. "Who will provide it for you? Have you thought of such matters?"

"Not really," Landon says.

"You all think you are immortal. No one prepares for death any more. You are all cowards, but death will find you and like a traveler in a foreign land your soul will get lost without a compass. Your life is meant for you to find map of the celestial planes, else it is all for nothing," Mr. Zhang says.

"You're talking about my soul, how it's gonna find its way home…"

"Yes, Landon. You are a horse in wilderness. American soul horse, yes? You need to find the way home, across the waters, you understand?" Mr. Zhang says.

"Like a Chincoteague pony," Landon says.

"I am not familiar with this Western concept," Mr. Zhang says, looking at his bodyguard for help, getting nothing. Mr. Zhang turns his attention back to Landon. "You were given many clues, but you followed none."

"How do you know that of me?" Landon asks.

"I know that of everybody. True for everybody," Mr. Zhang says.

"What clues?"

"Like advice, men gave you advice in your life, but you dense as a rock. Nothing gets through," Mr. Zhang says.

"What men?" Landon asks.

"Ordinary men. But the advice, not so ordinary. The advice it came from gods, Buddhas, disguised as ordinary men. The Buddhas, they sometimes speak from the mouths of ordinary men, women, or even children," Mr. Zhang says.

"A bit deceiving of them, don't you think?" Landon says.

"No, it is just *upaya kausalya*," Mr. Zhang says.

"Say again?"

"The doctrine of skillful means," Mr. Zhang says. "You received advice that conformed with your ordinary setting, yes? Incidents, episodes, they all appeared familiar, nothing special. But the messages, they were special."

"And I ignored all that," Landon says.

"You ignored all that once, you must *not* ignore that all over again. Concentrate, Landon, look at me. When you die, your soul, it leaves your body and finds itself lost in a realm of lights and images. From central realm, the All-Pervading Circle, a blessed Buddha appears before you, his body is white in color, he sits on lion throne," Mr. Zhang says.

Landon's mind reaches to a moment not so far back into his past. A scene replayed in front of him with uncanny verisimilitude and vividness. Just like when it happened in real life, but now with an additional layer of meaning that he'd failed to glean the first time around. There he was, Mr. Rocanna, dressed in an impeccable white suit, sitting astride his horse.

"What's his name?" Landon asked.

"The Lion's Den," Big Ben said.

A lion throne indeed, realizes Landon. And Mr. Rocanna's words, still stinging, could there have been truth to them?

"Same time," Mr Zhang continues, "under influence of bad karma and your impulse towards aggression you will be frightened and drift away, attracted by the light of lower realms. That's Day One. On Day Two another blessed Buddha appears from Realm of Complete Joy. His color is blue, he sits on elephant throne."

Landon harkens back to another day in the Arcadian fields, to that old fool Nick, dressed up in a sharp blue suit. *"Who do you got in second?"* Landon recalls asking.

"I'm riding on Elephant In A Room," Nick said.

Landon tries to remember what Nick said to him that day. It must've been important, but he missed the clues. Was he even paying attention? Would the Buddhas be ever so deceiving as to put words of wisdom in the mouth of that degenerate gambler? Not deceiving, maybe just desperate, an option as a last resort? Landon couldn't decide.

"But you will not recognize his wisdom, and so further you descend. Every day a different deity appears before you—," Mr. Zhang says.

In his mind's eye Landon is playing a video game with his son Tyler.

"You'll never get to the next level if you keep making the same mistakes," Tyler said.

Shit, they got a kid teaching him life lessons now? And what's with the tripe, *don't make the same mistakes*, it's just something people say all the time. Fuckin' fortune cookie wisdom. Nothing particularly deep about it. Was that supposed to jolt him into action? Or inaction? Okay, he has to admit, it did have weight coming from a kid, *his* kid. Maybe that was the whole point, a cliché coming out of the mouth of an innocent child. Or maybe it was something else altogether, like Tyler asking about the simulation game. How life-like it appeared to Landon at the time. There may be some truth to that, Landon has to concede. These series of flashbacks definitely feel like a simulation game, but how far does the analogy hold? Does it hold to life itself? Not sure. Will have to sit on that one. Landon's grasp of reality slips even further. The center cannot hold any longer.

"...A different deity appears in order to offer you choice and illumine the path of righteousness—," Mr. Zhang carries on.

Now here's Mr. Briggs Sr. lecturing Landon from the comfort of his peacock chair, only now his words break down and assume different shapes, some are barely heard, others jump for attention, associating to create a meaning Landon missed the first time around: drunk on Steven Gold's lies... he was... how you kids say nowadays, *money*... and Keith Brood, my first-cousin, my brother, *my family*... that corrupt monkey... while his Nameless True Friend was... a *Goddess*! Was Mr. Briggs trying to convey to his son the meaning of a parable all along? God, everyone's been lecturing this poor guy like they got nothing better to do. How's he supposed to get all this? Why don't they get off their high horses and mind their own fucking business? The nerve on these people.

"... But each time you choose wrong way—," Mr. Zhang says.

Landon flashes to the wrestling match with Ray on the floor of the hospital ward where Tyler rests in a coma. Damn right, I chose the wrong way, Landon says to himself. Shoulda knocked that sucker out when I had a chance.

"...Until the soul, by and by, recognizes the luminous path of innate wisdom," Mr. Zhang says.

"How long does this journey take?" Landon asks.

"It could be three days, it could be seven days, or even more. Who knows what sins you have committed, wandering in samsara," Mr. Zhang says.

"I'm so afraid... I'm always worried about my boy, y'know," Landon says. "I already lost a son, Jason, and this one is all I got left in this world. I never worry about what could happen to me. I've been around, went to war, I've seen things... after a while you think nothing can touch you. But now... shit, now you got me worried about my soul... Y'know, I've done bad things, which I regret, but there's also love and kindness in my heart."

"Love and kindness for who?" Mr. Zhang asks.

"My boy Tyler, my wife..." Landon says.

"It's easy for someone to show kindness to family. Not so to strangers," Mr. Zhang says.

"True," Landon says.

"And the soul, Landon..." Mr. Zhang leans in, points at Landon's pocket, and holds out his hand.

Landon reaches into his pocket and produces the object that triggered Mr. Zhang's anger. It's the Tibetan Windhorse that Landon, unbeknownst to all but its owner, had pilfered earlier that night. He hands it back to its rightful owner.

"The soul," Mr. Zhang says, as he holds the trinket up in front of Landon like a priceless artifact.

"The soul is a stranger in this world."

* * *

The limo arrives at the tall, fenced gate leading to the truck repair shop. Landon hears the driver's door open, then the clink of the keys in a lock, and the squeak of a gate opening. He braces himself, knowing that the guard dog, Cerberus, is protecting the premises at night but soon as the rushed footsteps of the Doberman approach, he hears the muffled sound of a gunshot and the final squeal of the unfortunate animal. It's a free ride to Hell from here on out.

Landon and Mr. Zhang walk up to the cigarette truck, their path illuminated by Lil Panda's bouncy flashlight.

The goon inserts a key into the lock and pops the back of the truck open.

Mr. Zhang grabs the flashlight and peeks inside at the covered pallets. He motions to Lil Panda, who jumps in with some ease for his size, hence his nickname, and uses a boxcutter to slice through the packaging until he hits the motherlode.

"Looking very good," Mr. Zhang says. He says something in Chinese to Lil Panda, who opens a cigarette carton and then waves at the limo driver to pull up closer.

"What are the terms?" Landon asks.

"The terms? That is not something you need worry about, the terms," Mr. Zhang says. He holds up a cigarette and the limo driver rushes over to light it up for him.

"I don't understand," Landon says.

"You really don't get it, do you, Landon?" Mr. Zhang says.

"Get what—"

Snakes of smoke curl out of Mr. Zhang's mouth and into the night sky. "You are dead man, Landon. You just don't know it yet," Mr. Zhang says.

That'd just about ruin any conversation, so Landon just stands there speechless and hoping that this whole affair has indeed been just a simulation game but, one way or another, he fears the worst.

"You don't believe me? Here, keep it," Mr. Zhang says, and he hands the Tibetan Windhorse trinket back to Landon.

"We even now," Mr. Zhang says, and proceeds to laugh and cough at the same time.

The back of the truck slams shut, echoing Death in the moonless night.

*"The Lotus Lord of Dance will appear
    dancing with a crescent knife
and a skull full of blood."*

The Tibetan Book of the Dead, Day Seven

Landon's voice is almost a whisper, a mumbling like a cascade of forgotten words to a plaintive song that no one dared to sing in ages for fear of awakening the gods of old. His voice goes quiet at last, but his fingers keep on strumming on the guitar for a little while, like they have a mind of their own.

Tyler doesn't appear to react to the song, he is still biding his time in limbo, connected to the physical world only by monitoring devices sending messages in combinations of ones and zeros, these machines unable for the moment to decide when to rest, like an ever-spinning ball on the roulette table, its final outcome predetermined yet unknown, either red or black, life or death.

Landon wishes he could get an inner sense for how Tyler is doing, but whatever the internal mechanism that appeared to automatically synch Landon up to Jason at a psychic level and beyond, is absent vis-à-vis his younger son. Jason, on the other hand, felt to Landon like a twin soul, like an offshoot of the same entity, two branches of the same tree, and even the smallest breeze or disruption in the air would not fail to affect one but not the other. The year before his death was a strange time in the Briggs household. The boy went through a dramatic change and Landon could pinpoint the exact date that marked the shift. Jason got into an argument with a boy at lunch break (it was over some girl, he later told Landon, without offering details), the argument turned into a scuffle, a no-no for someone in his condition, and soon Jason saw himself in a deadly headlock, dragged about the playground like a dummy to the amusement of the entire school. Something broke in him that day and the confident, articulate and funny kid everyone knew and loved turned overnight into a picture of submission and resignation. Whenever he'd run into his classmates on the street he'd lower his head and avoid eye contact, as if he'd been relegated to a lower caste. It killed Landon to see him like that but nothing he said managed to lift the boy out of his funk.

The burden of raising a family, taking care of a sick and moody child, dealing with rumors of infidelity on one side, gambling on the other, and sundry other problems had just about taken the fire out of the bedroom as far as Landon and Melanie were concerned. They'd fuck every now and then but just to remind themselves of the contract between them. But with the arrival of summer that year, and the endless succession of heat waves, there came a desire in Landon such as he hadn't experienced since high school. It caught Melanie by surprise, and she often wondered whatever had gotten into him. They were like in the early days, fucking everywhere in the house, finding ten-minute windows before tasks and errands to squeeze in a quickie. Melanie called it The Season of Lust. But the summer extended into the Fall, and then into Winter, and Landon at some point thought to consult a specialist, fearing his unusually frequent erections would take a toll on his health. One afternoon he saw the door cracked open to Jason's bedroom and he found the boy asleep in his bed. He drew close, then checked his breath, making sure it wasn't some fainting spell. The boy, about fourteen at the time, was just taking a nap though, his cell phone next to his body still playing a pornographic movie. Many things suddenly came into focus for Landon, like the long showers Jason started taking, the permanent "Do Not Disturb" sign hanging on his door (Landon forbid him from locking the door in case of an emergency), his sudden shyness around girls, and of course the source of Landon's unshakable lust by way of a sympathetic reaction to Jason's emerging adolescent libido. It was as if Jason was dragging Landon along through another puberty, warts and all. Landon had a talk with the boy later that day, explaining to him the ways he could go about relieving that pressure without putting undue strain on the heart, and the boy, red in the face, just nodded. Landon could hear him cry in his bedroom well through the night but there was nothing he could do to console him. Landon realized that a knowing had entered the spirit of the boy, a boy so sensitive to such things that he could not possibly miss the signals being sent from the beyond. Jason knew his time was at hand but couldn't express it in words, so he let his body suffer the burden of keeping that secret. And it all came to a head later that year.

***

Landon puts his guitar back in the case, as a slight draft gently blows the curtains surrounding the other Patient.

Landon digs into his pocket and takes out the Tibetan Windhorse, a present he sees as having arrived courtesy of both Mr. Briggs Sr. and Mr. Zhang. "This here's from your granddad, by way of a Buddhist something or other," he says, and he places the horse trinket on Tyler's pillow. At that moment Tyler's hand twitches. Landon places a hand over him and feels the warmth in Tyler's body and soon they start to breathe in unison, father and son, like synchronizing pendulum clocks.

Breathe in, breathe out.

Tick, tock. Tick, tock.

For once the two of them, father and son, fall in synch, allowing a subtle transfer to take place between them. But soon the perfect rhythm breaks into a syncopated dance when Landon hears a strange, otherworldly voice behind him, like a rainbow made of sounds. "Have you come here to mourn for the living?" the Patient asks.

Landon, startled and cautious, approaches the Patient's bed, his hand reaching for the partition in the drapes.

"You're crowding me," the Patient says.

Landon freezes in place. "Who are you?" he asks. He feels like he is speaking into a deep well, the reply coming only after the sounds have traveled into the abyss and back.

"I'm a messenger," the Patient says. "I'm far from home."

"What's your message?" Landon asks, intrigued. He peeks through the veil but can't make out more than the man's silhouette. He waits patiently for the answer. "It's been a long time," the Patient says. "I have forgotten it."

"Too bad," Landon says. "Wish I could be of help."

"I need you to do me a favor, now that you asked," the Patient says.

"Sure."

"I've been tied up to this bed for too long," The Patient says. "I haven't seen daylight in ages. I want you to walk up to that window." Landon can see the outline of an extended arm pointing to the window.

"Okay." Landon duly walks up to the window, like the man told him.

"I want you to look out that window and tell me what you see. Would you do that for an old man?"

"Nothing doing, man." Landon makes a few false starts, the words too timid to emerge out of his mouth and make a mark on the sensorial world. "I... I'm... I'm looking down at a beautiful park. The sun is out, a beautiful Cali day. I see people on lunch break, they look happy. Smiling faces, music in the air."

"Carry on," the Patient says.

"There's a young guy, early twenties, sitting on an apple crate, plays his guitar for no one in particular," Landon says. "Can't hear him from where I'm standing, but there's a couple behind him dancing to the tune so he can't be all that bad. His tip hat looks empty though, and he's got that look about him like he hasn't eaten in days."

"Another mendicant friar, is that all you have eyes for?" the Patient says.

"Gimme a break, man, that busker looks like an interesting character," Landon says. "You ask me, I'd like to know more about that guy—"

"What else do you see from your little watchtower?" the Patient says curtly.

"Wait," Landon says, "there's a woman."

"That's more like it," the Patient says, and his bed starts rocking back and forth like it's possessed. "Now we're talking. Is she beautiful?"

"Settle down, man. Yeah, she's beautiful all right," Landon says.

"What's she wearing?"

"She wears a flowery summer dress, high heels—"

"Is she wearing a bra?" the Patient asks.

"Yes."

"Nah. I hate bras," the Patient says. "What size?"

"Sorry?" Landon says.

"The cup, what size?" the Patient asks.

"I don't know, man, her tits are like ripe melons," Landon gestures. "They're bouncing up and down."

"Oh, I can almost picture that," the Patient says.

"Well, looks like she's pregnant, from where I'm standing," Landon says.

"Stay with her," the Patient says. "She interests me."

"Okay… She's walking up to the busker and drops some money in his hat. She says something to him, just a few words, and now she leaves," Landon says.

"Smart girl," the Patient says.

"I guess it wasn't money she dropped in his hat but some kind of note. He's reading it now. He throws his guitar over his shoulder and runs after her," Landon says.

"I don't see this ending well," the Patient says.

"Have a little faith," Landon says.

"Son, I ain't got nothing but."

"They're talking now," Landon says. "They're sitting on a bench and she's crying. He tries to comfort her."

"Is it his child, you think?"

"Of course it is," Landon says.

"It's a beautiful feeling, having a child, is it not?"

"Yes."

"Too bad it won't last," the Patient says.

"All things change. Nothing is eternal," Landon says.

"That's wisdom, right there."

"Buddha Shakyamuni's parting words."

"Yes, yes. In the end, everything will be forgotten, everything will be taken away from you," the Patient says.

Landon laughs.

"Did I say something funny, hoss?" the Patient says.

"No, it's just that until last night this wasn't something I was comfortable discussing," Landon says.

"They say that when you die your whole life flashes before your eyes. You believe that?" the Patient says.

"Maybe."

"You see those scenes, but with different eyes, not like when you first lived them," the Patient says, with the conviction of experience. "They're just thought forms projected onto the screen of a fake world."

"A goddamn *simulation* game?! Is that what it all comes down to?" Landon says.

"Much is at stake. Sometimes the gods speak through the mouths of strangers. But how can you tell?" the Patient says.

"I know, right?"

"Too late when you're dead already."

"I have a feeling we'll soon find out," Landon says.

"*You* first, dipshit," the Patient says.

"I get there before you, I'll lock up the place and throw away the key," Landon says.

"Oh, watch us then, the hungry ghosts, storming the walls of the Kingdom. And there ain't shit you can do about it," the Patient says. It's his turn to laugh now.

Tyler's eyes open for a moment then close again. Landon catches it like a flicker out of the corner of his eye.

He rushes to Tyler's side and plants a kiss on his forehead.

* * *

It's late evening when Landon makes it out to Stephanie's place for a routine welfare check after several calls to her went unanswered. He uses his set of spare keys to enter and is immediately struck by an ominous stillness. A stifling pressure builds in his head, nearly popping his eardrums, like the air is charged with fear.

It smells like Death.

It's been three years to the day since Landon last experienced something like this. He has desperately tried to suppress the memory of that fateful night in Tijuana, but it was simply a matter of time before it all came back with interest. He was still married to Melanie back then, though barely, and telling her that he was going on a trip south of the border to a town with a seedy reputation would have rocked the boat just enough to capsize it. So he kept the real purpose of the trip to himself. He told her he was visiting Ozone Layer, his old army buddy, at Camp Pendleton Marine Corps Base, just North of San Diego. He said he was going there with Frankie, and they'd be staying the night because they expected a shitload of reminiscing and drinking to be done and driving back to LA that night would be asking for a different kind of trouble. Melanie had heard the stories about Ozone Layer and naively bought into Landon's bullshit hook line and sinker, or else she did a great job pretending. It was the day before Halloween, and Landon promised he'd be back in time so that he and Jason would take Tyler out trick or treatin' for the first time. He wanted to spend Halloween night alone with the boys and the three of them had picked out costumes at a specialty store on Hollywood Blvd weeks before, in anticipation of the festivities. Landon was to be Dracula, Tyler chose a ghost costume, while Jason went for an elaborate Casanova getup. Landon balked at the latter, saying that Jason was perhaps a little too young to pull that off, at which the teenager replied that it was a way to face his greatest fear.

"What fear is that?" Landon asked, and Jason drew near to his dad and looked into his eyes and said, "That I'll die a virgin." Landon shook his head and whispered to him "You will live a long life, Jason, I know it. You will have a family, kids of your own," and then his voice began to break, as if his body was revolting against the mind's lies. Jason knew instinctively what it all meant as he begged his father, "Dad, just promise me you won't let me die a virgin."

"Of course I won't let you—"

"That's all I want, Dad, in this world. My only wish is that I don't die a virgin," Jason said, his own voice crumbling under the pressure of the moment. "Promise me."

"I promise you, son," Landon said. "You won't die a virgin. You have my word."

Jason was dry heaving as he held his arms around his dad, and barely got the words out, "Thank you, Dad!" while Tyler, not knowing what was going on, started to sob on his own while clinging to his older brother. One big mess.

Landon was clocking about ninety miles an hour on the I-5 South when they flew by Camp Pendleton the next morning, giving nary a glance to the base or even reminiscing about Ozone Layer, which the occasion might have called for. It did cross Landon's mind to bring it up, as a way to pay their respects if nothing else, but just as he was about to speak he turned and saw Frankie roll down his window and let fly a loogie that bounced off the asphalt like a skipping rock, and that just about killed the solemnity of the moment. Landon took that as a bad omen, seeing as Ozone had saved Frankie's life back in Iraq. As for Frankie, he was plagued by chronic pain for all eternity, it felt like, and relief came only in small measures thanks to the cheap drugs he was able to procure during his bi-annual trips to Tijuana. While other vets were able to adapt to the times and hustle some deals online on the dark web or even worse, Canada, Frankie kept to his Tijuana routine year in year out.

So when Landon joined him on his trip down South that year he just let Frankie lead the way, as it appeared he knew his way around town and was even able to break into basic Spanish, or as he called it, Mejicano.

They parked the car in an open lot on the American side and crossed the border by foot. Soon as they walked across the bridge into Mexico, Landon felt a certain unease, like a stifling he couldn't quite place. He felt like the sky hung lower there, as if someone had pulled a veil over the world, like a caul over the head of the unborn. He felt trapped in a metaphysical prison. He resolved in his mind to explore the possibilities of bringing Jason there on a subsequent trip, as to appease the boy's dire wishes to lose his virginity but a.s.a.p., and after testing out the waters himself, as it were, get out of that Tijuana pressure cooker as soon as possible. It didn't help that Dia de los Muertos was just a couple of days away and the celebrations had already started, giving the town an air of funerary masquerade.

A red VW Beetle, replete with driver, was already waiting for them on the other side of the bridge, which impressed Landon no end. "How you like this shit, huh?" Frankie said. "You ride shotgun 'cause you're my special guest, all right? And this here's our driver, Jorge. He knows all the good hookers in town, and where they live, disease-free. Don't you, Jorge?" Jorge, a middle-aged man in a sweaty flowery shirt, laughed a toothless smile and nodded politely. "He also speaks Ingles. Now, *andale, por favor,*" Frankie said, and they were on their way. That, by the way, was the extent of Mejicano uttered by Frankie during that entire trip.

Landon rolled down his window to let some air in, but he felt weaker by the minute, as if the draft was chipping away at whatever strength was left in him. The busy streets and tacky storefronts soon gave way to drab houses and poorly paved roads, and he wondered out loud where the hell they were going.

"Oh, we're just making a quick stop," Frankie said. "Won't take but a minute. Then I'll show you the good life."

The car came to a stop in front of a small house at the end of a long narrow street. No words were spoken between Frankie and Jorge, which made Landon believe that the whole thing was fairly routine. Frankie stepped out and knocked on the front door while Landon waited in the back seat of the car.

"Tonight is night of the *Angelitos*," Jorge said out of nowhere.

"What's that?" Landon asked.

"We celebrate the souls of the children who died, they come to visit on this special day."

"There's a day just for that?"

"Yes, it is special day if you lost a child, or someone you knew who died young, then the child can pay visit to you, yes?" Jorge said.

"But how?" Landon asked. "How does that work?"

"There is only thin curtain between this world and the other world, and on this day there is a hole in the curtain. Is like you open a door, and you look outside. Or inside because it is same, no?" Jorge said.

"I guess."

"When the spirit of the child comes, you will know," Jorge said.

Landon figured that he somehow landed in precisely the place that sort of thing would happen and probably did.

He peeked out the window and spotted Frankie talk to an old woman in the doorway. There was some shouting, but Landon couldn't quite make out what was being said. At some point Frankie reached into his pocket and pulled out a fat wad of cash, which he handed to the old lady. She took the money and went back inside, while Frankie waited impatiently, constantly turning in place. Presently, the door opened, and a boy stood there, about five years of age. Frankie grabbed his hand and brought him to the car.

The boy was quiet in the back seat and, as the car got rolling, Frankie read Landon's mind and said to him "Don't ask." With no need for further instruction, Jorge maneuvered his car through the busy roadways until they reached a convenience store, the kind where you could buy anything from toys to colon cleansers. They were there for the toys. Ten minutes later the boy emerged out of the store holding a bagful of cheap plastic pistols and Lucha Libre action figures, but if he was happy with the presents he chose not to show it. A quick and quiet trip back to the house then an awkward farewell between Frankie and the boy completed the side trip. They had barely left the house when Frankie started sobbing like a bitch alone in the back seat. After five excruciating minutes he said, "That was my son, man... My *boy*. I'm gonna bring him to LA soon as I get my shit together, you watch."

Landon could hardly believe that someone he thought he knew perfectly well as a world-class big mouth could hide such a secret from him for so long, and he reminded himself not to be too quick to judge. Also, what else was the fucker hiding from him?

Next stop was a strip club in the Zona Norte part of town, *la zona de tolerancia* as the locals call it, and Landon wasn't about to stage a protest even though he was hurting to get to the motel, take a shower and let the new revelations settle in. But TJ wasn't done with him just yet. The joint was on the main drag, Calle Coahuila, and Landon got a sense of the spirit of the place well before they reached their destination. Cheap hookers lined up the sidewalks and crowded the corners under the gaudy neon signs lit up well before sundown, moving crookedly on their high heels as if on stilts, every gesture in slow motion, forcing time itself to grind down to a slower pace.

"Looking for a good time, mister," Jorge said. "Yes?"

"Yeah, y'know, I heard that the Tijuana Cultural Center is not quite what it used to be, so..." Landon said. He spotted a girl, couldn't have been older than Jason, looking like a waxed clown in her makeup and blonde wig, her aged-beyond-her-years eyes tracing Landon like laser beams from behind the fake eyelashes.

"You have eyes on thee *las paraditas*?" Jorge asked.

"What's that?"

"*Las paraditas*, you see them, yes," Jorge said, pointing out at the street hookers, "I like *las paraditas*," he laughed. "Very spicy, you understand? Cheap, too. Jorge get you one girl, thirty dollar. She come to your room."

"I don't know, man," Landon said.

"You want two girls? Fifty dollar," Jorge said.

"Take it easy, Jorge," Frankie cut in. "We've just entered the reservation. The man's trying to save his bullets for the bigger game. Not like they gonna be running outta pussy anytime soon, know what I'm saying? Besides," he said as the car came to a stop, "here's the best game in town."

The strip joint bore the unlikely name of Hong Kong, and occupied the lower levels of Hotel Cascadas, a tall, by TJ standards, red building.

"This is us," Frankie said. "Meet you down in the lobby in ten."

Landon checked into his hotel room, just quick enough to clean up, remembering not to accidentally drink the tap water, bring a measure of respectability to his appearance and rush down to the lobby to meet Frankie. He didn't know what the rush was all about until they entered the strip club.

Frankie greeted the burly doorman with an open hand, a twenty-dollar bill smoothly transferring from one hand to the other. "Johnny," he said to the doorman, "this is my best bud, Landon. Su casa, *his* casa, or however that goes."

"Good to see you, Frankie," Johnny said, his accent sounding more like East L.A. than Tijuana.

"How's things?" Frankie asked.

"Same 'ol, same 'ol. You'll get a kick outta this," Johnny said. "Last night, this loaded businessman, some kinda Asian, tailored suit, slick back hair, the works, dropping cash left and right, he in the middle of a lap dance, Florita's right on top of him, like this," Johnny paused, and moved his hips lusciously in a circle, "and y'know Florita, she can work it til it drop, well, the gook keels over, face plant, like he was about to eat her out or something, but no, he was having a fuckin' heart attack. He die right there, bro, buried in pussy."

"Well, if you gonna check out, can't think of a better way," Frankie said.

"I mean I always knew Florita's the best, but hell…" Johnny said.

"What'd you do with the guy? You try to give him mouth to mouth?" Frankie asked.

"Oh, fuck that shit, bro. I ain't touching no motherfucker. I just dragged his ass out here on the sidewalk. Federales picked him up," Johnny said.

"That's cold."

"Standard operating procedure. It's Hong Kong, bro," Johnny said, then pointed to the stage as a dancer came on to a Spanish cover of California Dreamin'. Landon caught the tail end of the DJ's intro, telling them to open their pockets for Carmen Carnal.

Frankie dragged Landon to an open table, where margaritas appeared seemingly out of nowhere, along with a round bottle of Tequila Mandala. The sultry dancer worked through her routine like there was only one client in the house, Frankie. The whole show was for his benefit, and the horny frat boys and businessmen lining up the front row that girdled the stage held tight to their purse strings seeing as, in her eyes, they counted for nothing more than pesky mosquitoes. For once, the veil that usually covers such transactions between entertainer and patron was pulled right open and the implicit suspension of disbelief that allows the imaginary erotic attraction between the parties involved to move currency from one pocket to the other suddenly broke like a spell. Carmen was quiet the looker but, to Landon, her caramel skin, her petite features, and especially her eyes, just slightly wide apart, reminded him not of the spicy Latinas of his dreams but rather of the boy he saw earlier in the day. He had no doubt that dancing in front of him was the boy's mother, Frankie's baby mama. He looked into his wallet for a ten-dollar bill as her routine was winding down, not sure what the protocol required in situations like that, tip or no tip, but Frankie was quick to cut him off. Oh well.

Soon as the song ended Frankie rushed backstage and there he stayed, lost somewhere in the belly of the beast for the remainder of the night. He gave Landon no explanation. It was one of those things.

Just a couple minutes later a lissome stripper, golden G-string, D-cups coming up for air, approached Landon's table and gave him a hug like they'd known each other for a lifetime.

"I am Florita," she said. "You with Frankie, yes?" she asked. "Yes! He say, hey, that's my fren over there." She laughed. "So, you buy me drink or what?" Before Landon even had a chance to reply, she motioned to a waitress holding a tray of drinks, like it was New Year's Eve, to bring some of the good stuff over. Landon reached for the bottle of Mandala, but she was in the mood for Champagne.

"Florita, you said your name was?" Landon said, "I heard you had some guy croak on you the other night."

"Oh, I am famous now," she laughed, "Now everyone want to know what is my secret. It is good for the tips."

They clinked.

"So what's your secret?"

"I didn't kill him, the Japanese," Florita said. She took a sip of the potion. "He was here for two weeks, he stay here, coming down here every night, throwing away his cash. Big tips, you know?"

"High roller," Landon said.

"Yes, but he tol' me one night, he say, I am going to die any day," Florita said, putting on her best sad face. "All this money, it is my savings. I don't need it. I come here to die, he say."

"What a strange thing to say, huh," Landon said.

"Yes, very strange man. When I dance with him, every night, I hear him say the same words over and over," she said, swaying her hips in a hypnotic dance ever closer to Landon. She placed her wrists on Landon's shoulders, not grabbing him, just letting him know she's there. "I don't know what they mean, I think maybe something in Japanese," she said. "I ask him, but he don't say. He just keep saying them. Now I keep hearing those words in my mind, because I hear them so many times, you know, but I don't know what they mean," she said.

"What were the words?" Landon asked.

"Namu amida butsu. Namu amida butsu," she said. "Do you know?"

"Namu amida butsu?" Landon repeated. "I'm afraid not."

"So do you want to party?" she asked, perhaps remembering that time waits for no one, and, in fact, time is money. "I finish here in one hour."

Landon agreed to her terms and conditions, as far as money (couple hundred, because inflation), time (an hour guaranteed, maybe a little more, because fren of a fren), and the use of condom (yes) and orifices (no anal, but fingers and/or tongue okay, because she high end), and then he gave her his room number.

After a quick shower he looked at the watch and saw that there was still half an hour to burn, and he could already feel the high of anticipation. He parted the blinds and looked out onto the street. The sun had gone down, leaving in its wake just a pink strip over the horizon. The city was coming alive, though in a way Landon wasn't familiar with. A mariachi band strolled down the middle of the street, its members wearing grotesque masks, looking like they'd crawled out of their graves just a few minutes earlier, replete with accordions and cymbals. Bringing up the rear of this horror show was an inordinately tall and slender man, wearing his suit like a coat rack, and on his hand he held the leash to a wild burro painted to look like a zebra. Precisely what the meaning of all this was, Landon couldn't tell, but a sadness overwhelmed him at the sight of the beast of burden made to look like a zoo animal and he wished that donkey was stubborn enough to suddenly change its mind and start to walk *backwards*.

The caravan ruckus was fading in the night and Landon heard some catcalls. A young prostitute was staring straight at him from across the street, whistling, twerking her tiny ass and waving her arms up and down, her dress making her look like a winged demon, or perhaps like a bird of Paradise during mating season. No matter, Landon's mind was still with the poor donkey, and he shut the blinds.

This is when the call came.

At first he thought it must have been Frankie, asking for a favor or for company, and he'd made up his mind not to answer but when he saw that it was Melanie he picked it up. He sensed that something was amiss and braced himself for the worst. He always had a knack for feeling out the varied misfortunes coming his way and all signs pointed to something grim.

What followed will forever be a blur to Landon. Years later he tried to recall exactly what was said but was never able to. He remembered the grotesque sounds of the street amplified to a deafening level, the catcalls of the teenage hooker, the cry of a baby, the thump of the club downstairs, an empty bottle rolling down the sidewalk below like the order of the universe was upturned and he alone could hear all the cries of the world. The enormity of the news was like a power surge to the system. It crushed and crippled him for life.

His beloved son, Jason, was dead.

Landon dropped to his knees, numb, mumbling something to the extent that he'll try to get back home as soon as possible. He hung up and realized he'd forgotten to ask how, why, where, when. It didn't matter. His boy, his flesh and blood, was gone. He had to get back home but his fingers couldn't move to push a button on the phone. He sobbed, his face buried into the musty, stained carpet. At last, he managed to pick up his cell phone and call Frankie, but there was no answer, so he left a message and called right back again. And again. The deafening roar in his ears was subsiding and he sat on the edge of the bed to try to get his senses back, not knowing where he'll get the strength to get up again.

He took a few deep breaths, something he'd learned in the army, and the moment he closed his eyes he felt that familiar warmth at the root of his spine, the current surging like electricity through his body, causing him to stand up like a rod, nearly jolting him out of his shoes. It was the same sensation that first overcame him in the hospital waiting room the day Jason was born.

It was unmistakable. This was Jason come in spirit form.

His boy was there in the room, inside Landon's body somehow, on the night of the *Angelitos*, and Landon could feel the pressure coming from all sides, his hairs standing on end.

Landon heard a knock on the door, which startled him out of his wits. He peeked through the door viewer to see Florita standing there. He'd forgotten all about her. He managed a flimsy thought, an excuse to send her away, somewhere along the lines of "here's full pay for your trouble, thanks but I need to leave, it's an emergency." However, there was an erection standing at attention in his pants, telling him he was no longer in charge of his body, and like a divining rod it was pointing straight at the whore.

Landon sensed the urge intuitively and remembered, or rather he was made to remember, a solemn promise he'd made to his son. That he was not going to let him die a virgin.

There was no time for small talk and the foreplay amounted to Landon giving the whore sloppy open-mouthed kisses all over her face and down her neck, the booze in her breath turning him on like a new perfume. He helped her undress, all the while pulling his own pants down, making sure the condom rolled snugly on his member, and soon he was naked right on top of her.

"You horny bad boy," Florita whispered in his ear, "you want to fuck this pussy," and he nearly came right then and there.

He entered the whore and started to thrust, slow at first, but then fast accelerating to a fever pitch, and between the sounds of the flesh slapping against flesh he heard the moans of the whore approaching climax, and he instinctively reached for her nipples, twisting the two knotty mounds hard like a *torsades de pointes* until she pushed her pussy back into his groin and he came like a bill in the mail. He rolled over, sweaty and confused, yet strangely exhilarated, staring at the ceiling like there was a hole in the sky.

"Papi, you fuck like jackrabbit… like teenage boy," the whore said. "I mean in good way. You make me cum good."

"This was my first time," Landon said. "I was a *virgin*."

The whore laughed like it was the funniest thing she'd ever heard. "You want to go again, is okay, virgin boy."

But Landon passed, as he could no longer feel his son inside his body, or in the room for that matter, his spirit having left with the orgasm and the fulfillment of his wish. This was an experience Landon never shared with another living soul and while there wasn't a day in his life he didn't think of his dead son, he never again felt his presence. Landon spent many days and nights wondering if Jason's visit was real. He wanted confirmation after-the-fact but didn't get it and, as time passed, the possibility of that whole experience having been just a figment of his imagination gathered steam in his head to the point of driving him insane with guilt.

* * *

Now a few years removed, as he enters Stephanie's apartment, Landon gets that stifling sensation again, like the ghosts were calling him out of a thousand mouths. The kitchen looks like it's been vacated in a hurry. Dirty plates stacked up in the sink, crumbs on the floor. The TV is running on mute in the living room. It shows a wildlife documentary, two wild mustangs fighting for breeding rights in Devil's Garden, California. The door to the bedroom is open and soon as he peeks through, Landon knows.

The sight of Stephanie and Frankie sprawled out on the bed doesn't come as a shock to Landon, just a mild disappointment. They are both naked under the blood-red sheets, looking like they've just had sex.

They've also just been murdered.

Hanging on the wall, above the headboard, is a blood-splattered painting of Kali, the Hindu Goddess of Death and Liberator of Souls.

Landon stands at the foot of the bed, seemingly unable to process all the information. He moves closer to the bodies, touches Stephanie's face. He drops down to his knees and does the only thing he could possibly do this late in the game. He asks the gods for forgiveness.

"What have I done?" he repeats like a mantra. "Please forgive me. What have I done?" But he is crying as much for his friends as for himself, having realized that his fate is sealed and there's no going back now. What's done is done. He tries to get up but can't. He feels a suffocating pressure in the room, like an invisible army is trying to cram inside. There are spirits around him, of that he's certain, and he can sense his dead friends almost touching his face. They have come as messengers and Landon can hear their thoughts like screams from the beyond—

"We have traveled to the Wooden House in the Green Valley, where we saw your son, who was once a boy and is now a Man."

And just like that a breeze blows through the room and it is quiet again, and Landon knows deep down in his heart that his boy had become a man that night, even though in death, and he understands that whatever his mission was in the journey of that soul, it ended that night in Tijuana. A sense of freedom takes over Landon and his own soul appears to be buoyed by a wave of anticipation, like a homecoming, which propels it past the confines of the body and Landon finds himself hovering over the city in search of Tyler, a beacon of light pulsating a few miles away as the crow flies.

Tyler's hospital ward is chilly, and a Nurse pulls a red sweater over her hospital scrubs. She parts the drapes to the Patient's bed and helps him onto a wheelchair. He is none other than the Traveler who has been stalking Landon of late, or else his evil twin.

The Traveler has on a psychedelic shirt, with a rainbow of colors splattered on it in a spiral shape. He has long silver hair in a ponytail reaching down to his ankles; a traveler out of the Sixties, or out of time perhaps. As he sits down in the wheelchair, he places his ponytail on his lap like a pet snake.

"Roll me up to that window please," the Traveler says.

The Nurse rolls the Traveler to the only window in the room and parts the drapes. A shaft of light casts an ethereal glow on the patient.

He looks out the window to see tall buildings on all sides, with no open view to a park or anything else for that matter.

"God, that's a view fit for a brig," the Traveler says.

"This is not a resort, sir," the Nurse says.

"Where's the goddamn park?" the Traveler asks. "I don't see a park."

"There's no park, sir," the Nurse says, surprised. "What in the world made you think there would be a park?"

"Never mind. I would tell you if I thought you'd understand. But I don't. You understand?" the Traveler says.

"Do you need more time, sir?" the Nurse says, as she checks her watch.

"God, no. Just get me the hell outta here," the Traveler says. "But quick."

The Nurse spins him around like a top and the two head for the exit.

"I can't wait to see this world I've heard so much about," the Traveler says, and starts whistling a wistful tune, an even sadder version of the one Landon had played to his son Tyler earlier that day.

The Traveler vanishes as if he's never been there. Melanie gasps as Tyler's eyes open at last. It takes him a few moments to get his bearings but is comforted by the sight of the familiar face.

"Oh, Tyler," Melanie says, covering him with kisses.

A nurse absentmindedly cleans up the bed next to them, somehow incapable of erasing the imprint left on it by the Traveler, unaware of the miracle taking place just inches away from her.

Tyler clutches his mother's hand. "Mom?" Tyler whispers, as the face in front of him comes into focus.

"Yes, my boy, it's me," Melanie says.

"Tell me a story," Tyler says.

"What story would you like to hear? Something from your books? Apollo and Daphne? Orpheus and Eurydice?" she asks.

"Tell me how you and Dad met," Tyler says.

"We met at a park. I was on lunch break, walking back to my office downtown. I was in a bad way... Not something you'd understand, but anyway, I caught a glimpse of this young man, your dad, strumming on his guitar in the center of the park... he was playing a beautiful song, I remember it to this day," she says. "But that was a long time ago... before Jason was born. When he finished his song he asked me to meet him at some park downtown, under the Clock Tower. We made a date."

"Why there? Why at the Clock Tower?" Tyler asks.

"I don't know," she says. "I think it was on account of a dream he once had, but he never told me what the dream was."

* * *

Landon finds himself strolling aimlessly at first, crossing a street when the light is green, or turning either left or right if the light in front of him is red, as if in a maze of his own making. He left Stephanie's apartment in a daze, with the full intention to put some distance between him and the scene of the crime, knowing that it was only in the physical that this were at all possible. He needs breathing room to process what just happened and plan his next move. He cannot stop, not even for a moment, for fear of hitting an actual dead end, like his whole body would just come crashing down to a full stop right there in downtown, the center of the labyrinth. Walking down 9th Street against the flow of traffic Landon arrives at the tiny green oasis with the unlikely name of Great Hope Park. A flood of memories comes rushing in as he approaches the spot where he had his first date with Melanie. He looks up to the Clock Tower still standing there, the paint chipping off on the sides. It looks nothing like the one he'd seen in his dream, but then reality has always appeared to him like a cheap imitation of some higher state, the worldly equivalent of a Made in China knockoff. Which only goes to show, he figures, the topsy-turvy nature of things.

Indeed, there in the middle of the green lawn he spots a group of three elderly Chinese women practicing a type of qigong, their movements slow and soothing, like caressing the wind. Landon feels a sudden and inexplicable urge to approach the group and he takes his place beside them and starts imitating their movements. One of the women stops for a moment and places Landon's arms in the correct position. He syncs his movements to theirs and tries to empty his mind of all thoughts, but one image persists. It is a wheel of fire that turns over his head, and with it turn the ages of man, and history is reduced to fractions of a second, and Landon can see that lives upon lives fly off the edges of the wheel and dissolve in the abyss, body and soul, and he feels a deep desire to find a place on the arms of the wheel—if not now, then in the future, and remain there while whole worlds teeter on the precipice.

When he finishes, he turns to the elderly woman and asks, "What do you call this move?"

"Buddha Stretching a Thousand Arms," the woman says.

* * *

Landon finds the truck parked where Mr. Zhang had abandoned it after gutting it of its cargo. Lil Panda gave Landon a call that morning to let him know that he can have his truck back and where to find it, just a couple blocks away from his lair. This was a rare gesture of affection from his boss, who had taken a shine to Landon after dreaming of him the night before. Lil Panda didn't tell him what Mr. Zhang's dream was all about, but Landon took it as a sign pointing to the end of the road.

Landon steps up in the driver's seat of the truck and closes the door behind him. He puts the key in the ignition, ready to turn. He stops and reaches for his cell phone. He first places an anonymous call to the police, to the effect that shots were heard coming from Stephanie's apartment and wouldn't someone care to come take a look.

He then dials another number.

It rings and rings. Finally he hears the familiar outgoing voicemail greeting. "It's Melanie. Only leave a message in case of an emergency."

"Hi, Melanie. I just called to tell you that I'm sorry for everything. I love you, and I love Tyler, and that's all I can do," Landon says. "It's all I can do."

He hangs up and gets the truck on the road.

An hour later he pulls up in front of Lex's warehouse just as the sun is about to set. The door to the warehouse opens, and out come Ray and Lex. Landon pops the back of the truck open.

Ray turns on a flashlight to reveal an empty truck.

Landon hands Ray a plastic bag containing several bricks of cash. Ray looks like he just got handed a dead cat.

The men walk silently back into the warehouse, where Landon is quickly surrounded by four super twin goons, each coming from a different direction. They all wear Diadora tracksuits of a different color: green, red, yellow, and white.

"Landon, meet the Diadora brothers," Ray says.

In perfect synchronicity the brothers pull out crescent-shaped knives.

"Time to balance the books," Lex says.

The brothers circle ever closer to Landon. Ray takes out a wallet-sized photo of their dead brother, the Runt, and flashes it to the brothers, says "Vedi?" The Diadoras respond, *"Vidi, vidi."*

Landon appears serene, at peace with the world and his fate.

His sense of sight is suddenly displaced and through the small, greasy window of the main door he could spot, if so inclined, the shapes of men coming together for what appears to be a dance of sorts, a ritual so savage it could only have damnation or salvation as its ultimate goal. The shapes come together then pull apart, like they all breathe together as a group, until they don't.

The earth suddenly starts to shake with a force only Mother Nature can conjure. The big sign over the exit door comes crashing down to the ground where it shatters in a million pieces.

The lights start to flicker, then go completely dark.

There are rumblings and strange sounds approaching, like all the wildebeests were let loose on the world.

This is no ordinary temblor.

This is the Big One.

EPILOGUE

For the first time in years Tyler had a dream that night. He dreamt of a small herd of wild horses venturing off an island and into the shallow waters leading to a foreign shore about a mile away. Tyler locked in emotionally, as one would in a dream, to a scared little pinto patterned pony bringing up the rear. It tried to keep up with the herd but found the waters intimidating. At some point the little pony came to a stop in the middle of the channel, not knowing which way to go. Tyler, with all the mighty power of his dream mind, comforted the pony and urged it on. At last, as if hearing the boy's beckoning call, the pinto patterned pony took heed of its surroundings and caught up with the rest of the pack on the shoals, water splashing over its frail body all the way up to its neck. Dry land was just within reach, and it looked like it might make it after all.

THE END